Un-Friendly Persuasion

A Quaker Mystery

Chuck Fager

Kimo Press

Special Thanks to:

The Writer's Support Group at Pendle Hill; and
The Delaware Valley Chapter of Sisters in Crime; and
Asa David Leonard Fager,
for help in identifying Northern Virginia's finest
Western Fries;

and, of course,
The United States Postal Service,
Without which none of this could have happened....

NOTE: With the exception of historical references, and Postal Regulation 661-56, this story is entirely fictional, even the parts I wish had happened. Although, to tell the truth, I did knock over a whole row of mailboxes once.

ISBN 0-945177-12-7

First Edition

Kimo Press
P.O. Box 1771
Media PA 19063

In memory of

David E. Eppers,
of Salem, Massachusetts and the world;
Samuel and Miriam Levering of Ararat, Virginia;
And E. Raymond Wilson of Washington, D.C.

CHAPTER ONE

one

When we heard the 7:30 mail truck backing into the dock, Merle left his sorting case and headed for the door. "Come on, Perry," he called, "I wanna show you something."

Reluctantly I closed the copy of the new catalog called *Victoria's Secret,* shoved it into the slot for Kasabian on Bluebird Lane, and followed him.

It was no wonder the casing of mail slowed down whenever these catalogs came in. They were meant to grab our attention. The models' nipples showed under the lacy bras and hair tinged the vees of their shiny panties. Satiny, semi-nude couples lounged on every other page, looking as if they didn't know each other's last names but had been doing it for hours with wild abandon. Ever so elegantly, of course; and having just rested and freshened up a bit, they were now ready to go another elegant ten rounds or so.

Despite the obvious artifice, I found the whole thing sexy as hell. As, apparently, did most of South Fairfax's postal customers.

"What's up?" I asked when we got outside.

It was cold on the dock; February in northern Virginia and winter had finally decided to pay us a visit. A brief one, I hoped, as did all sane mail carriers north of Florida. All but the closet sadomasochists, that is; but they had mostly been promoted to postmaster anyway.

Merle lowered his voice. "You wanted to get in on one of the pots, didn't you? So now's your chance." He waved at the driver, a pudgy type with sunglasses and an unlit cigar sticking out under his beat-up Postal Service cap, walking carefully up the icy ramp. "Hey, Fred, how's the mail look

1

today?"

"Nothin' much, Merle," answered the driver, "just the usual junk and garbage." When he got closer he took the cigar from his mouth and his voice dropped. "What you got for me?"

"Another player," Merle said. "Perry Adams, new RCR. Wants to get in on the payroll pot."

"No problem." Fred shook my hand and flashed a tobacco-stained grin. "New RCR, huh? How you like carryin' mail? Gone into the ditch yet?"

I opened my mouth, but he didn't wait for an answer. "Just gimme a quarter and any four-digit number. The number turns up in the Maryland Lottery next Friday, you win the pot. It's no big deal, couple hundred bucks maybe, but it comes in handy."

"Four digits?"

"Yeh," Fred said. "Whichever ones you want. Maybe even"--he pointed his cigar toward the parking "--9998."

I squinted past the chewed stump toward the navy blue Subaru which bore that number on its plate. At my elbow, Merle guffawed.

"That's Ferris's car," he said. "9998 is the new plus four add-on for a postmaster's Zip Code. He wants the world to know what he is."

"Really?" I snickered. "What's the code for bastard?" They grinned again. "Okay, put me down for 1211; my birthday is December 11." I dug for a quarter.

Fred spoke to Merle. "You got any more for me?"

"Hell, yes." Merle reached into the breast pocket of his plaid flannel shirt, and pulled out a postal buck slip, on which I could see a handwritten column of names and numbers. "This's the ones from here and down at the American Legion too. Lotta them guys--"

"Is that what I think it is, Merle?"

It was Mr. Ferris. The postmaster had come up quietly behind us. Now he stood over us, glowering. "I've had just about all the crap from Merrifield that I need about cleaning up illegal activities on postal property, and this is gambling, sure as hell."

2

Ferris turned on his heel and opened the back door. "I want you and that paper in my office, Merle. You, too, Adams."

"Christ," Fred said, scratching nervously at his right ear. "Guess I better get the hell outta here. And just for the record, Merle, I don't know nothin' about any pot. I thought you was giving me some phone numbers for the spring bowling league."

"Sure," Merle muttered, "cover your ass." Fred retreated gingerly down the frozen ramp. Merle shoved the sheet back in his pocket. "All right," he said to me, "let's go face the music."

Behind us, Silas the clerk was pushing a big All-Purpose Container full of mail sacks off the truck. The APC looked like a miniature jail cell on wheels, and it clanged as it hit the concrete dock.

"Merle," I whispered, "what can we get for this?"

"Aw, hell," he growled, pushing back an American Legion cap from his shiny forehead, "Ferris thinks he'll get promoted, and have some new asses to kiss. I'll probably get wrote up. 'Don't bother me. I'm ready to retire anyway. But you could get fired, if Ferris really wants to make points with Merrifield."

He shrugged. "Sorry about that."

"Hey, thanks," I muttered grimly.

Just what I need, I thought. Fired as a substitute mailman after three months on the job. It's not like I need the money or anything. It's just what's keeping me out of jail. Damn Heidi and her slick alimony lawyer anyway. Not to mention the tenure committee in the English Department at Arlington County Community College.

Ferris's office was next to the front counter, and as we passed it some big lady customer was giving Andy, the window clerk, a hard time. "My mail hasn't been gettin' delivered til sometimes as late as six o'clock," she was saying, poking a thick finger at him. "Yesterday it was all mixed up with my next door neighbor's mail--again. And my Social Security check is three days late."

Merle grinned back at me. "Mrs. West," he whispered. "Late for her monthly appointment at the liquor store. She knows how to raise royal hell when she misses out on her drinking.''

Andy listened to her impassively, chewing his gum and nodding slightly. I saw him glance up at the wall clock as we went through Ferris's door. Andy was a short-timer, and without doubt he could have told us exactly how many days, hours and minutes were left until his retirement.

Ferris was on the phone, rubbing his creased forehead with two stained fingers, between which a cigarette burned. He looked old enough to be my father, paunchy and with a harried expression. He surely was old enough to retire; probably had retired once already, I figured, from the military, like Merle and Andy and half the other Post Office lifers. Today he looked like he ought to do it again.

''Yes, ma'am,'' he said tiredly into the mouthpiece, ''I'm sorry about that. We've had substitutes on that route a lot recently, and they're not as familiar with it as the regular carrier. So you're right, the delivery service hasn't been as good or as fast as it should be lately.'' He sucked on the cigarette.

Go ahead, I thought. Blame it on the sub. That's why you hire us RCR's in the first place: to take the rap. I just hoped he wasn't talking to someone on Route 66.

There was a loud knocking on the other office door, the one leading to the lobby. Ferris ignored it, took a quick pull on the cigarette and stubbed it out in an ashtray. ''Yes, ma'am,'' he said again, ''I'll speak to him about it, and if we can't get your service improved, somebody will be out of a job. Thank you for calling.'' He coughed and grimaced. ''And have a nice day.''

He hung up and rubbed his forehead again. ''Christ,'' he said to no one in particular, ''that General Kelly's wife on Bald Eagle Court is gonna drive me crazy if we don't get her mail right pretty soon. And the general knows a lotta bigwigs who can cause us trouble, too.''

I felt a twinge of relief. Bald Eagle Court was on Route 89, the one Herman Corson, the other RCR, had been struggling with. So I was off that particular hook.

But now Ferris had focussed in on Merle and me, and remembered why he had called us on the carpet. He tapped

4

another cigarette from a pack on his desk. "Merle," he said, pausing to light and suck on the cigarette, "I've warned you before about this gambling. I don't give a damn what you do on your own time, but you know you can't do it here."

He picked up a memo from the desk. *"'Employee Regulation 661-56,'"* he quoted: *"'No employee while on property owned or leased by the Postal Service while on duty will participate in any gambling activity.'"* He glared up at Merle, and continued: *"'This includes the operation of a gambling device, conducting or acting as an agent for a lottery or pool, or--'"* his eyes moved to me-- *"'selling or purchasing a numbers slip or ticket.'"*

He dropped the memo. "That just came down from Division headquarters at Merrifield. They're serious about putting a stop to this crap. So I'm gonna have to take action this time." He pointed at Merle's shirt pocket. "Gimme that sheet; I wanna see what's on it."

As Merle's hand moved toward his pocket, the knocking came again, louder and more insistent this time. "Christ," Ferris muttered again. "Just a minute," he said to us, got up and stepped over to open the door.

It was Mrs. West, and she started right in on him. "Mr. Ferris, where's my Social Security check? It's three days late." The thick finger was pointing again, a bit shakily.

Merle's hand dropped back to his side. Looking down at Ferris's desk, I noticed that, lo and behold, right by his phone, only a couple feet from me, lay a whole pad of buck slips. And the top one was blank.

An idea flashed into my mind; it made the palms of my hand tingle. With Ferris at the door, there were only a few seconds to act on it, if I was going to.

I went for it. I tore the top sheet off the pad and folded it down the middle. Then I plucked the other sheet from Merle's pocket and replaced it with mine. Crumpling up the original, I looked frantically around for a wastebasket and didn't see one.

"Yes, Mrs. West," Ferris was saying, "I'll look into it personally, right now. You wait there, and if it's in this office I'll bring it right out to you."

5

Still no wastebasket, and time was up. I stuffed the wad of paper into my mouth and started chewing.

It was dry and tasted bitter. Full of toxic chemicals, I thought. Lead, mercury, probably arsenic.

Ferris had turned and brushed past us to the inside door. "Herman," he called, "we should have gotten a Social Security check for Mrs. West on Hideaway Lane. Look in that backed up mail and see if you've got it."

I tried to swallow the paper, but it made me gag. My eyes started to water, and I could feel my face flushing. On a second try, the wad went down, but then I felt like I was going to choke and went into a coughing fit.

"Something wrong, Adams?" Ferris asked, back in his desk chair and pulling again on his cigarette.

"I-uh," I said weakly; there was very little to my voice. "It's--why, it's the cigarette smoke, sir." I hacked noisily. "Irritates my mucus membranes." The best defense is a good offense, right? We'd soon see; I was desperate.

He stubbed out his cigarette. "Yeah. Sorry." Then he stuck out his hand again. "The paper, Merle."

Merle handed it over. Ferris unfolded it and saw it was blank. He looked up at me, his eyes narrowing, then at Merle. "You smartass sonsabitches," he hissed.

"Mr. Ferris," Merle said brazenly, "I know how you feel about gambling, really I do. I was just gonna make Fred a list of some people who are interested in the spring bowling league, that's all. He'll tell you so hisself."

Herman tapped timidly at the door behind us. He was short, round, with eyes that bulged slightly, long greasy black hair and a vaguely unkempt look. Merle was sure he was gay--a faggot was his term--and the older carriers studiously ignored him unless it was absolutely necessary to speak to him.

Right now he wore a sheepish expression. "I think I found the check, Mr. Ferris," he said. "It was in with a stack of sweepstakes letters." He shrugged. "Looked just like 'em."

Ferris got up and snatched the envelope from him. "Christ," he repeated, dismissing Herman with a wave, and turned back toward the outside door. Then he stopped and glared

6

back at us. "You guys think you're pretty damn smart," he said. "The inspectors' gonna have your ass one o' these days. Now get outta here and get back to work."

He opened the door and we left. Behind us we could hear Mrs. West's shrill voice turn to mollified squeals, as visions of thunderbirds and wild turkeys danced on the envelope she now held in her wrinkled paw.

"Gotta hand it to you," Merle said to me, "that was pretty slick. They'll get a laugh outta this at the Legion tonight. Guess I owe you one."

I just nodded, since I still couldn't find much voice, and walked back to my case. There were four feet of letter mail left to stick on Route 66 before I could pull down, get out on the street, and, if I was lucky, stop by Jennifer's and get it on.

two

There was another knock at the office door shortly after Perry and Merle left. Walter Ferris sighed again, swiveled out of his chair, reached for the handle, and paused for a few seconds, breathing deeply, struggling to recover something approximating a friendly, professional demeanor.

But this time when he opened the door, his reaction was an honest smile. "Lemuel Penn," he said warmly, "come on in. What the hell brings you to South Fairfax?"

The man in the door smiled back. "Well, Wally," he said, shaking Ferris's outstretched hand, "what does thee think? Business and pleasure, as usual."

The visitor wore an outmoded brown suit, and his shoulders were slightly stooped. When he took off an old fedora hat, his thin hair was more sparse than Ferris remembered. But his eyes were bright and piercing, and his carriage had an air of natural dignity. He shuffled into the office, looked around it, and then sank onto the narrow metal chair Ferris pulled for him from a corner.

"The pleasure, of course, is seeing thee again," Penn went on. "Though there is something a little bittersweet about it too." Penn reached into the sagging pocket of his suit coat and

7

produced a small leatherbound Bible, its cover worn and weathered.

Ferris leaned back in his chair, feigning alarm. "You're not gonna preach at me, are you, Lem?" he objected. "Sunday was yesterday, you know, and I'm still not a churchgoer anyway."

"No," the visitor protested, "no sermons. The Lord will have to tend to thee Himself." Penn opened the book. "I merely used this to transport something for thee."

"What--" Ferris stopped, as his visitor reached into the pages, then handed him a small bundle that was small and bell-shaped and delicate.

"Yes," Penn said quietly. "It's been uncommonly warm in the Valley this last month, and they came early."

Ferris gazed at the dainty ovals of snowdrop blossoms in his rough, aging palm, pressed flat by Penn's Bible but still shapely, ivory-colored, and exquisitely out of place in the bureaucratic jumble of manuals and forms and old coffee cups strewn across his desk. The only touch of empathy amid the debris was a framed photo of a woman with a beehive hairdo, just past the bloom of youth, holding a grinning child in her arms.

Without looking up, Ferris moved his other hand across the desk toward the photo. A half-eaten bagel smeared with cream cheese sat somewhere near it; he fumbled for the thick paper napkin it had come wrapped in.

His fingers found the napkin. He raised it and wiped at his eyes. "Twenty-two years," he whispered.

Penn nodded. "Yes," he said quietly, and his eyes too were shiny. "Yes. Thy Emily and my Sarah. Still asleep on their hillside. And it was my turn to bring these. This time, though, it also has to do with business."

Ferris was only half-listening. He couldn't remember how long ago their private ritual of exchanging snowdrop blossoms had begun. He and Penn had grown up near each other, on apple orchards in Martindale, on the western slope of the middle Shenandoah Valley. But they had not been close friends, and still weren't, at least in the way of camaraderie.

But where life had not connected them death did,

indissolubly, in early 1963, when cancer took both their only daughters, barely a month apart. Just as spring was beginning to be rumored in the Valley, the young women had been laid in the cemetery behind the Martindale Regular Baptist church, down the winding road not far from the orchards where their fathers had been raised.

Neither man belonged to the church, but that hadn't mattered. Penn's Quaker meeting was farther down the Valley, and had no cemetery; Walter was un-churched. But if the Martindale Regular Baptist congregation was small, its grounds were large; and what their compassion didn't cover, the lot fees did.

Then, sometime in the early seventies, the two men had met in the cemetery one early spring afternoon. Penn was carrying an improvised bouquet of snowdrops, the kind that were blooming in 1963, and offered to share them with Ferris. Since then, each year for more than ten years now, they had met at about this time, and one had brought a sampling of snowdrop blossoms, the kind that were blooming then, to the other.

Last year, it was in early March, Ferris had found himself suddenly drawn to take a day's leave and drive west in I-66, then south on I-81 past Harrisonburg to Martindale. He found the opening buds he had somehow known would be there, picked a few sprigs, then visit Penn's place up the road.

This year, he hadn't thought about it til now. But it wasn't his turn.

This gesture was something Ferris had never spoken of to another person, and he doubted Penn had told anyone either. Yet he felt sure it would probably continue, year after year, as long as either of them could travel. And after that, there was always the mail. Always, the mail.

Something Penn had said came back to Ferris, jarring his reverie. He looked up from the white petals. "What do you mean," he murmured, "these have to do with business this year?"

"Thee hasn't heard, I expect." Penn was unfolding a sheet of paper, which he placed on the desk. It was a fuzzy xerox of a newspaper clipping from the *Valley Times*. *"Federal Prison*

9

Slated for Martindale Area," was the headline.

Ferris leaned over to read the article, and his forehead creased into a frown. "A prison?" he asked. "There?"

"Three hundred fifty acres they want," Penn was saying. "They tell us it'll hold six hundred. More likely they'll stuff a thousand in it, same as all the others. It's a crazy idea, bad for everybody, the inmates and the town. County Chamber of Commerce is all for it, naturally. Most everybody else is against it. They asked me to come down to visit Congressman Abernathy, see if I can stop it. I've got a petition."

He put several sheets, stapled in the corner, on top of the clipping. The top sheet was covered with scrawled autographs on neat columns of straight black lines.

Ferris pursed his lips and leaned back. "I can kinda see both sides," he said. "There's jobs and supply contracts to be had, the Chamber would like that, and the county needs 'em. And we do have to get these criminals off the streets. Been too soft on 'em too long."

He paused. "But on the other hand, there goes the neighborhood. And damn it, it's my neighborhood. Or used to be. Still think of it as home."

Penn was nodding now. "I know we don't see eye to eye much in politics, Wally. I imagine thee's still sold on Ronald Reagan, voted for him again last November?"

"Over Mondale?" Ferris huffed. "That was easy."

"For some," Penn replied evenly. "But even so, this rush to build more and more prisons is self-defeating and mean-spirited." A passionate note crept into his voice. "It shows our society's refusal to take the domestic effects of war and poverty seriously." He raised the bible and his voice deepened. "Like it says in here, we reap what we sow. What we need is drug treatment and job training--"

Ferris had raised a hand, and was shaking his head. "No sermons," he repeated. "Remember?"

Penn gave him a resigned smile. "All right. But maybe we can at least agree that they ought to put this, er, institution, somewhere else. Martindale Regular Baptist voted unanimously against it. It's no wonder, since the plan calls for the outside wall

10

to run smack up against their cemetery property."

"What? A prison wall?" He stroked the snowdrops with a calloused finger.

Penn nodded. "Razor wire," he said. He watched Ferris's lips compress. "Armed guards. Spotlights."

"No," Ferris said decisively. "That's too close to Emily." He reached for a black government issue ballpoint. "I don't know about the rest of it, but I'm with you this time, Lem." He pulled the stapled sheets toward him, scribbled on a blank line.

But then he raised a sudden finger. "Just don't think this makes me one o' your liberal do-gooders. I better not start getting junk mail from the ACLU."

He winced and corrected himself. "Er, I mean *bulk* mail from them."

"Don't worry," Penn smiled. "I've known thee long enough to have no such illusions. This list goes nowhere but to the Hill."

He stood up and grasped the fedora. "I should be gettin' into town," he said. "There's a markup scheduled on the authorization for this prison late this week or next, and I better bend some ears up there before then. And in the meantime, I'm to give a talk to the Adult Class at the Washington Friends Meeting."

"Oh, yeah?" Ferris asked. "On what? No--let me guess." He feigned concentration. "Bible study?"

Penn smiled faintly. "Wisdom."

"Wisdom?" Ferris needled. "D'you have any?"

"Not much," Penn said. "But this does." He tapped the pocket with the Bible. "Proverbs and Ecclesiastes. Those are my texts."

"Sounds interesting," Ferris said, without conviction. He stood also, and shook Penn's hand again. The firmness of Penn's grip belied the sense of fragility about him. "Give me a call when you've been up to the Hill," Ferris said. "Lemme know how it goes."

Penn put on his battered hat. "I'll do that," he said.

three

A man in a black overcoat and a Russian-style fur hat stood on the curb of Independence Avenue in front of the Air and Space Museum. Peering east, he saw a grey Mercedes driving down the slope past the Rayburn House Office Building. It pulled to a stop a few feet from him, and the passenger side window slid down.

"Need a ride, Sergeant Hanrahan?" the driver asked.

Hanrahan stepped off the curb, slipped on the ice, recovered himself and got in.

"So where were you, Gil?" the passenger said as the car pulled away. "I been waiting there for fifteen minutes. It's cold as hell."

The driver shrugged. "Shoulda worn your uniform, George. I hardly recognize you without it. Been by here once and didn't see you. My eyes aren't as good as they were back at school. Anyway I had to take the long way around, to be sure no one was following me."

The driver placed a small envelope on the seat. "Here. This'll warm your ears up a little."

"Hey," said the passenger, picking up the envelope. He opened the flap and thumbed the sheaf of twenty-five twenties. "Another contribution to the St. Joseph's Military Academy Alumni sailing club," he said. "How about that; my boat's almost paid for, Gil."

He slipped the envelope inside his coat. "You're right. I feel warmer already, old buddy."

He stared without interest at the Washington Monument, its ring of American flags fluttering weakly on their poles. Ahead was the grey bulk of the Lincoln Memorial, rising from a tangle of leafless trees. Beyond it, sunken in its permanent grief, the mirrored ebony of the Vietnam Veterans' Wall.

"Okay," Hanrahan said at last, "this is it: The chairman has definitely decided to run for the Senate next year."

"Shit," commented the driver. He turned the Mercedes left at seventeenth Street, circling back along the Tidal Basin toward Interstate 395, towards the Fourteenth Street Bridge.

12

"So he wants the investigation to produce some indictments," Hanrahan went on. "Get his name in the press and all that, the sooner the better. And he's hired this new chief investigator, Phil Gibb, some hotshot from the Denver D.A.'s office."

"Know anything about him?"

"Only that he got the job after he nailed a bunch of city workers and contractors for kickbacks out there. And that he's been on the phone a lot to the Justice Department Criminal Division."

"What are they talking about?"

"I haven't been able to hear that much of it, Gil, but I think I got the drift, and it ain't good. The bottom line is gonna be to hang a few smaller subcontractors out to dry--"

"You mean, like me."

"--Yeh, like you, and let the biggies slide past."

"Of course. The bastards."

"Yeh, well, you see, that way it works out to everybody's advantage: the administration is in with the biggies up to their keister, whatever that is. Going after the top contractors would not be embarrassing. For that matter, it might throw a wrench in some of their favorite projects, like the MX or even Star Wars. The chairman is no big fan of either one, actually. But the big guys cover their tracks so well it'd take five years and a brigade of investigators to really nail them."

"But Chairman Abernathy doesn't have five years to run for the Senate, right?" the driver asked rhetorically. The Mercedes was on the George Washington Parkway now, with the Pentagon behind them and Arlington Cemetery to their left, its ranks of white headstones poking up through the remains of low, wind-smoothed snowdrifts. On the other side, chunks of ice swirled in the muddy Potomac.

O'Connor eased the car into the left lane, up the ramp towards Memorial Bridge. "And since the real sharks like United General," he said, "are too damn much trouble, he'll settle for the balls of a few small fry like me. Look, George, what have they really got on me so far?"

"I don't see everything, Gil, but somebody has been feeding them what looks like copies of invoices, and they've been

13

checking them out. I've heard the staff talking about it: Billing for six guys when there were only three, and working twelve hours at overtime rates when they were only there eight, charging for fancy pistols and communications equipment that never showed up, stuff like that. You know, Gil, you haven't been very sophisticated about it all.''

"Sophisticated?'' O'Connor demanded. "Who needs sophistication? For four years there's been so much money coming down you needed buckets just to collect what was slopping over the side of the trough, which is all I've been doing. Of course, I'm not sophisticated, George, I'm a goddam amateur at this. Your boss wants to see some serious business, though, I can tell him who the real pros are. I've got their phone numbers.''

The Mercedes had crossed Memorial Bridge, curved behind the Lincoln Memorial, and was headed east on Constitution Avenue.

"Maybe that's what you should do, Gil, go to the chairman. See if you could make a deal, point the finger somewhere else.''

O'Connor tapped his fingers on the steering wheel; his leather driving gloves sounded almost like wood in the quiet auto. "George,'' he rumbled, "I've already got a lawyer, and he costs a lot more than you do. You're a cop, and a friend. I'm paying you for information, not advice. Anyway, don't think I haven't been trying to figure out how to cover my ass. And I have some ideas. It may not be as easy for them to nail Gilbert O'Connor as they think.''

The monumental columns of the Archives slid silently past, and beyond the sharp angles of the East Wing of the National Gallery, the Capitol loomed before them.

"So what about subpoenas?'' O'Connor demanded.

"Nothin' yet,'' Hanrahan replied. "Don't worry, you'll be the first to know. You gonna want to talk again next week as usual?''

"I'll call you,'' O'Connor answered. "I might be going out of town for a few days. Think I need a little vacation, some time to think. But I'll be back soon enough, and I'll want to stay on top of this stuff. Especially if there's talk about subpoenas.''

"Yeh, well, be sure you only talk about the Alumni Association when you call. I don't trust any of the phones on the Hill.''

"No problem. You want out at the Russell Building?''

"Yeh, I'll get some lunch there and take the tunnels back over to the House side; they're warm and dry.''

The Mercedes pulled noiselessly to the curb at the corner of Second Street. The sergeant got out. "See you," he said.

O'Connor waved, the door clicked shut and the car pulled away.

Hanrahan watched the car until it turned on Fourth Street, headed back towards 395. Then he reached into his coat, to the inside pocket where the envelope full of twenties rested, next to a miniaturized microphone hookup.

"You got all that?'' He said into his armpit. "It should be enough. I'm gonna get something to eat over here, and then I'm going to the seminar room for the lieutenant's test prep session.''

As he finished talking seemingly to himself, an old man came up to him.

"Excuse me,'' he said, "but can thee tell me how to get to Congressman Abernathy's office?''

"That's on the other side,'' Hanrahan replied. "But you don't want to walk in this cold. I'll show you where the subway is, it's faster and easier on your feet.''

"Thank thee, Friend,'' the old man said. "I'm much obliged.''

four

"Perry, be sure and check the numbers before you sign,'' said Silas the clerk repeated as he handed me the clipboard. "Losing a red is a big deal. You could even go to jail.''

I dutifully checked the numbers on the red stickers on the two checkbook-sized boxes, compared them with those written on the record sheet, and signed it.

Silas is a natural pedant. I don't say this as a putdown;

15

it takes one to know one. He would have been a teacher for sure if he hadn't flunked out of college. These days, especially with RCRs, he couldn't just give you a piece of accountable mail, without volunteering a lecture of greater or lesser length to explain its significance and hazards. The other carriers made fun of his earnestness when he wasn't around, but I didn't mind it.

"Registered mail," he went on, "travels under lock and key, and with armed guards if necessary. In the bigger offices, like up at Fairfax, it's kept in a locked area called the Cage. Everyone who handles it has to sign for it. The driver who brought it had to sign, I had to sign, and now it's your turn. And when you get back you've gotta have either the red or a signed 4936.

"A what?"

"The little yellow slip. If you don't bring back one or the other, you're looking at a possible ten thousand dollar fine and a stretch of federal time, courtesy of the Postal Inspectors."

Ah yes, the Inspectors; the Postal Service's own miniature FBI, our Little Big Brother. Other people only hear about them when they break up mail fraud scams, or bust somebody for soaking the cancellation marks off stamps to resell them.

But postal workers know that the Inspectors spend most of their time, not watching criminals, but watching us: Checking to see if we're stealing mail, throwing stacks of junk circulars in a dumpster somewhere, taking money out of envelopes, or selling dope to each other.

One of the most fascinating parts of orientation at the Division offices in Merrifield, at least for me, was when an Inspector came in. Surveying the rows of newly-minted city carriers, clerks, mailhandlers, rural carriers, and us few Rural Carriers Relief, he explained about the network of enclosed catwalks that ran just above our heads all over the inside of the building, like some kind of concrete rib cage. I hadn't really noticed them before, nor the little one-way observation slits in them every ten feet or so. But sure enough, they were everywhere.

The catwalks, he told us, were for the Inspectors, so they could keep an eye on us. There are special concealed entrances

16

to the catwalks too, so Inspectors can come and go without anybody knowing. Clever. You'll find the catwalks and the eye slits in every post office, except the smaller ones in rented space, like South Fairfax.

For my money, though, spending an eight-hour shift staring out those slits at the likes of us must be just about the most boring job of all in the Post Office, and that's saying something. But the Inspectors think of themselves as an elite unit, all college-educated and well-paid, and the rest of us are scared of them, or learn to be.

And don't think that without catwalks of our own at South Fairfax we're getting away with anything.

No indeed; Silas had assured me that to keep tabs on us they simply send people in undercover.

"For that matter, Perry" Silas had confessed to me just a week ago, "I figured *you* were an inspector when you started."

I laughed and asked why.

He flushed a little, and admitted that it was my tweed pants that made him suspicious. A little too cultivated for your average Rural Carrier Relief.

Actually, it was a good guess; I think I'm the only one at the station, including Ferris, with a college degree, and the pants were originally part of my junior professor costume. Meant for wearing with a tie to meet my classes, not for delivering mail. But they were warm.

Our business done, I took the reds back to my case. The address was on Bluebird Lane: Gilbert O'Connor. I slipped them into the tray of parcels in the proper sequence.

The clock showed almost one PM. Jennifer's kids got home around four-thirty. If I hurried through my luxurious ten-minute lunch hour, and didn't get stuck in the slush somewhere, we could have time for a hot midafternoon quickie. I had to stop there anyway, to deliver a certified letter. As Silas had also briefed me in detail, losing a cert was not as big a deal as a red; but you had to get them signed for on the yellow slip just the same.

It's funny how many certs Jennifer had been getting lately.

17

I smiled to myself. Funny, but not surprising.
After all, I had sent most of them myself.

five

O'Connor parked the car in front of the big garage, and went under the yawning raised door to the kitchen entrance, stopping first at the answering machine on the end of the counter. Its red light was blinking; there were messages. Just as he was hoping, and for one in particular. He pushed the replay button.

The first voice was familiar, but not welcome. "Gilbert, where's the check?" it demanded.

Ruthie, the bitch.

"If it isn't here by tomorrow the next call will be from my attorney. Or maybe I'll come over and get it myself. Don't try to pull this crap on me again, Gilbert. You know I won't stand for it. I--"

He hit the Fast Forward button, and her complaints dissolved into a short high squeal. Screw her, he thought. She'll be looking for more than her damned alimony check in a few days.

The tape crackled again. "Mr. O'Connor?" it was Ray, the manager of O'Connor Security Services. "I've got last month's time sheets for you to look at. We need to get them taken care of before they go to United General. I'll bring them by tomorrow afternoon. See you then."

That would be today, O'Connor figured.

The time sheets, of course, were where most of the creative accounting had gone on. And Ray was beginning to suspect that the company was under scrutiny, and wanted to make sure the boss signed off on everything, so his ass was covered.

No problem, Ray, O'Connor thought. They don't want you; they want me. They're chicken to take on United General. But on the other hand, if they're willing to settle for you when I'm out of reach, old buddy, that's okay by me. Unless, of course, it's you who's been giving copies of the invoices to the subcommittee in the first place....

The next voice was young and female. "Mr. O'Connor,

18

this is Susie at New Adventures Travel.''

This was somewhat better. O'Connor recalled Susie, of the large white teeth and the large, doubtless similarly alabaster breasts. ''Your reservations to Miami and San Jose are all taken care of,'' she said brightly. ''All you need now is your visa and you'll be ready to go. You can pick up your tickets at Dulles. If there's anything else I can do for you, just let me know. Bye.''

Yeh, he thought, there is something else you can do for me, Susie honey, but not at your desk. And he already had the visa, with his passport in his travel case.

The digital readout indicated one message left. It better be the one he was waiting for.

The background noise level on the tape suddenly picked up; long distance. ''Mr. O'Connor, Art Blumstein in New York here.

A sigh of relief; this was the one he'd been waiting for.

''We've gathered that investment information you wanted, and our report is in the mail. You should have it today or tomorrow. If you have any questions about it, please give me a call.''

Finally. Blumstein, the crook, had to be one of the slickest moneyscrubbers in Manhattan. And he was careful, too. In only six weeks he'd turned over a million dollars worth of O'Connor Security Services' assets into a packet of cash and bearer bonds. Half of it was coming in the form of his ''report'', along with a key to a safety deposit box. And Art had done it all so quietly it would be a month or two before anyone noticed the money was gone.

He rewound the tape to listen to Susie's voice again. But this time his reverie was directed more at her message than her remembered anatomy:

San Jose, that beautiful compact city with its climate of eternal spring; San Jose, capital of Costa Rica, a country whose government was honest enough to make life comfortable, but corrupt enough to provide extended protection from extradition to visitors who could afford it. And last but not least, San Jose-- home of the Banco Central Costarricensa, in one of whose safety deposit boxes the rest of Art's ''report'' would be patiently

19

waiting for O'Connor and his key.

The only thing O'Connor had worried about was getting the packet here. "I don't think I can come to New York," he had told Art. "I could be followed. And if you send a courier they may be watching the house too."

"No problem, Gil," replied the unflappable Art. "We'll just send it registered mail. The mailman comes to your house every day. He won't arouse suspicion. And registered mail is handled carefully; it will be safe."

"Jesus, it better be." O'Connor was nervous about having that much loose money laying around a post office. But Art was right; it would be the route least likely to draw attention. And there was no way to eliminate risk entirely from his plans, not any more.

Well, no use bitching. Time to get moving.

He went into the master bedroom. The king-size bed was unmade, the side table littered with a pizza container and beer cans. His desk, covered with paper and flanked by filing cabinets, stood at the far wall, next to the triple-paned glass doors that opened out onto the patio.

The patio overlooked his five acres of oak and a few maples, through which he could see the column of smoke from a chimney on Commonwealth Lane. The maid service had kept the rest of the place in reasonable order since Ruthie left, but he had told them to stay out of here. Too many sensitive items laying around.

His travel bag was in the closet. He flopped it on the bed and zipped it open. An issue of the *Tico Times* from last summer fell out, a remnant of his first trip to San Jose. O'Connor grinned at it and tossed it onto the bed. What was that gal's name? Antonia--or that's what she called herself for him, anyway. She knew how to party all right; he'd have to go looking for her when he got back to the San Jose Hilton. Just be sure to bring along a couple gross of Trojans, Gilbert, right? We don't need any itchy tropical diseases, now, do we?

Which reminded him. Ruthie's diamonds were still in the safe. Take them along too; If Antonia didn't properly appreciate them, some other brown beauty would.

20

He walked to the wall and pulled the corner of a large framed certificate from St. Joe's. The frame turned on the hinges, revealing the round door of the wall safe, with the keypad next to it. O'Connor pulled a credit card-sized piece of plastic from his wallet, inserted it into the slot under the keypad, punched in a series of numbers, and the safe door clicked. He opened it, reached in for the box of jewelry, and considered which of the pieces to take.

He rubbed his chin, and it scratched. He should shave before he left. He closed the jewel box and tossed the whole thing into the travel bag. The electric razor was still in the bathroom.

He heard a noise at the door while he was pulling the aspirin bottle out of the big medicine cabinet. The mailman? Ruthie? But then again, it didn't sound like the front door.

He swung the medicine cabinet door shut slowly and looked into its big mirror.

"What are you doing here?" he said.

six

Let me tell you about dogs.

Before I started as an RCR on Route 66, I used to like them; old Fluffy and me were inseparable for years when I was a kid. And one of the best things about Heidi, for that matter, was Harry, her somewhat sheepdog mutt. But Harry died, the marriage broke up, my contract at Arlington Community wasn't renewed and here I was, delivering mail out of my car, and along with these other changes my attitude toward dogs has recently altered considerably.

Most of the time I didn't worry about getting bitten. That's more of a risk for the city carriers, walking their routes. But when I did have to get out, to deliver a parcel or get something signed for, then I'm raw meat. Besides which, the dogs here can smell a mailman at least a block away, even in a car, and they're resourceful. Also devious and dangerous.

There were several on Route 66 who made life interesting. Take the schnauzer at 4225 Trotting Horse Circle,

21

Andersons. The beast was kept on a chain connected by a ring to a cable strung across the front yard. I had an express for them last week, and that little son of a bitch guarded their sidewalk like he was the last Marine at the Embassy in Beirut.

I tried to go around him but he stayed with me, moving right and left along the cable to keep me at bay, barking and showing those teeth. He was determined to get a piece of me. I honked and hollered, but nobody showed at the door, so I left. The Andersons did not get their express mail that day, and to hell with them. I'm a mailman, not a goddam SWAT team.

But the real killers were a pair that live at 2302 Bluebird Lane, just around the corner from Jennifer's. They're a South African breed, I think. Leastways their owner, Kasabian, was always getting mail from the South African embassy; maybe he's a lobbyist. His pets looked like a cross between Dobermans and German Shepherds--pointy ears, brown and black short coat, but thicker in the body than the Doberman.

I soon began calling them the Nazi dogs. The colors fit, and there was a kind of imperious malevolence that shows in their beady eyes when they watched me approaching Kasabian's box. It was a nonchalant, condescending kind of arrogance that I'm sure I've seen in pictures of Himmler and that Third Reich crowd. Or maybe the pictures were of the South African security cops chasing after blacks in Soweto. Sometimes they bayed at me from behind their fence, an eerie wailing barking that made hairs stand up on the back of my neck.

Anyway, since they usually couldn't get at me with their teeth, their idea of sport was to try to run me off the road. They did this by sitting down right in the middle of the street directly in my path when I was pulling back up the slope from the bottom of the circle. Bluebird Lane is narrow and curved, so I had to swerve to avoid them sitting there, and then they began to lope along beside me as the old Malibu wagon labored to accelerate up the hill.

Then they liked to play with me, veering from the side to right in front of the car, sometimes so close I couldn't see them over the hood.

All this, yet they never barked when they were on the

street. They tried to kill me without making a sound; it was almost eerie. They almost sent me over the edge a couple of times, too, braking to avoid hitting them and starting to skid.

You could get hurt that way, too. There were only five houses on Bluebird Lane, four on the south side and O'Connor's in the cul de sac, all with plenty of acreage. The shoulder dropped away sharply on the north side, not a big slide, but enough so the car would roll a couple times before hitting the trees and sinking into the pond at the bottom.

No big deal, really, just enough to kill me and maybe start a fire, giving the Nazi dogs a thrill as they watched, tongues pink and damp, eyes yellow and cold, while I tumbled and burned, then drowned.

That's how it goes in my nightmares, anyway.

A couple of times I've resolved to run these canine fascists down, but haven't quite had the nerve. I did try to squirt them once, with the mace they give us for just that purpose. That was when I had to take a cert up Kasabian's big U-shaped driveway that winds past a manmade pond with a fountain in the middle to get a signature.

I'd already tried to avoid going up there by just leaving a notice in the box; but Kasabian had called the station and told Ferris he'd been home at the time and insisted on redelivery, as did Ferris.

But either my aim was bad or the mace didn't work, because the dogs just shook it off and made another couple of their unnerving silent lunges. So Kasabian didn't get his cert that day either--I wouldn't have opened my door without first laying down a barrage of automatic weapons fire.

Today I was lucky. Kasabian's gate was closed, the Nazi dogs had to trot along parallel to me from inside the fence, and there was nothing in his bundle that needed to be signed for, just the usual junk mail--

--Oh, excuse me, I must remember that we are now under orders always to call it *bulk business mail,* if you please--

--Plus the normal right-wing fund appeals, and another newsmagazine from Johannesburg.

I stuffed them in the box, slammed the door up and shut,

and glanced back over the seat at the parcel tray, to check on what was coming up next, before my certs for Jennifer.

Oh yes, the two reds, for O'Connor at 2306. No dogs there, fortunately. Just a big house on a rise, at the top of another flattened crescent driveway; he had the end of the lane all to himself.

Big houses are nothing unusual out here. But most of them, when they have any recognizable style at all, mimic somebody's half-remembered notion of colonial Williamsburg or, closer at hand, the columned mansions of Middleburg's hunt country, which is twenty or so miles, and about as many millions, to the west.

But O'Connor's place made me think of California: white stucco with red adobe shingles and lots of tall potted succulent plants showing in the big windows. A flagstone walk led up to a wrought iron gate which looked into an enclosed patio. The flagstones crossed the patio to a big glass front door with more decorative wrought iron.

One afternoon last month, during the January thaw, I brought a parcel up his drive. It had rained the night before, and the grass down the lane and around the rise looked newly green. As I came up the long flagstone walk, mist was steaming up from the ground. With the warmth of the day, the subdued green of the lawn and the white stucco of the house, I could have sworn I had stumbled on Brigadoon in Northern Virginia, as designed by an exile from Marin County. Nobody was home that day, and I lingered for a few minutes, just savoring the scene.

Today, though, there was a crusty coating of snow on the rise, ice on the drive and the sidewalk, and a Mercedes parked in front of the big garage. So I got out, left the wagon running and the door open, stepped carefully on the flagstones, and rang the doorbell at the iron patio gate.

The big glass door opened and a tall man came out. He was in shirtsleeves and was wearing suspenders that held up expensive pinstriped suit pants. He hurried down to the gate, but didn't open it.

"Registered mail," I said, waving the parcels. "Need your signature."

The cold didn't seem to bother him. He fingered his empty shirt pocket. "Got a pen?"

"Yeh, somewhere" I said, handing him the parcels and digging into my pocket. There had been a pen in there yesterday. Heidi always hated the way I kept so much stuff in my pockets. But what else are they for, for chrissake? I found the ballpoint and gave it to him.

He looked at the green return receipt stapled on each envelope. "Which line do I sign?"

"Lemme see," I said. He handed the boxes back through the bars. Then I realized that the DELIVER TO ADDRESSEE ONLY box had been checked.

"Mr. O'Connor?" I asked, handing them back. "I'm sorry, but the sender wants to be sure I delivered them to you personally. Do you have any identification? Drivers license is fine."

"Sure," he said, and reached into his back pocket. "Damn, wallet's in my jacket. Just a second."

He turned and walked quickly back into the house. I waited, feeling the cold seep into my toes and fingers. I stuck my hands deep into my jacket pockets. It seemed like it was taking him a long time to find his jacket.

I heard talking inside the house, or was it shouting? O'Connor came to the glass door again, and started to open it.

And then somebody shot him.

I heard the shots. Holes appeared in his shirt, the glass door crazed as the bullets struck, and then collapsed as he staggered into it.

In the same instant I reflexively jumped backward, slipped on the icy flagstones and went down. Shots were still being fired, and above me the wrought iron gate suddenly clanged and quivered.

My head hurt. Jesus, were they shooting at me? Had I been hit?

I could still move, though, and scrambled on my hands and knees toward the back of the wagon, to put its bulk between me and whoever was shooting. I made it around the rear end, under the magnetized rubber sign that read CAUTION

FREQUENT STOPS.

The letters, I was thinking dazedly, are black, four inches high on a yellow background, per Virginia regulations. I was also very aware that though my head still hurt, there wasn't any blood dripping on the snow.

The firing stopped. I was crouched by the left rear wheel, and could hear what sounded like footsteps on the walk. But the gate was still locked, and maybe that would give me enough time for a break. Thank god that, contrary to regulations, I had left the car door open and the engine running.

I sprang forward and ducked into the wagon, grabbed the wheel, popped the brake and let it move on its own, steering with my left hand and not daring to peep over the dashboard.

But the car started to slide almost at once and I had to look. The wagon was headed for the ditch at the bottom of the drive.

I braked and steered to the left, and took another quick look. It was still sliding. Bullets or no bullets, I had to sit up and drive the damned thing.

I braked and steered and then hit the gas, and the rear end fishtailed back onto the drive. There was one last shot and some bark flew off a tree as I passed it. I flinched, but then I was out of the drive back onto Bluebird lane, which had been well-plowed and gave me some traction.

The wagon speeded up, past Kasabian's, where the Nazi dogs were still stuck behind their fence, watching me patiently, jaws wide and breath like smoke, confident that their turn would come, and probably soon.

I rubbed the back of my head where it hurt. No blood, no bullet hole, just a bump from when I fell. Instead of feeling relief, though, that was when I started to shake. My hands were trembling so much that I almost didn't make the turn at 3903 Fox Run Shoals, into Jennifer's long steep driveway.

CHAPTER TWO

one

Philip Gibb hung up the phone and pondered the Day-Timer that lay open on his desk.

His hair was a bit longer than was the norm for The Hill, his tie looser and his navy corduroy suit more rumpled. But the handwriting on the datebook's left-hand page, under the Heading TO BE DONE TODAY was precise and clear. There were 17 items on the list. It was after three o'clock, and items 1 through 14 had thin, angular check marks beside them, indicating their completion.

Not bad, Gibb mused, but he knew he'd better hustle if he was to get through the other three, and finish the day with a clean slate. He didn't worry about his appearance much, but he hated to leave the office without check marks beside all the items on the TO BE DONE TODAY list.

But there was a hassle with item #16, he could see. It read: Set up Stakeout on Subject, Ffax.

O'Connor. The talk this subject had with George Hanrahan today, even broken up when the car went under bridges, left the clear impression that he was going to make a run for it. That could be a real problem.

We need O'Connor, Gibb mused. We need to scare him into talking about his little security guard contract scams. And then scare him some more, enough to start talking about what some of the bigger crooks from United General he was subcontracting from were into.

He would know enough about that to point them in the right direction. And provide some dramatic testimony, the kind of stuff that looks great on the tube. Maybe even enough to produce an indictment or two. Enough to keep it going until the

27

campaign was finished and the chairman had moved up to the Senate.

And who knows, maybe even send a crook or two to jail for ripping off the public till. That was a long shot, Gibb knew. But there was always the chance. And O'Connor was their main prospect.

But not if we can't get him on the stand, he thought. And to do that we have to give him a reason to stick around. Like a subpoena. Gibb tapped his fingers on his desk, in the space between the neat stacks of papers and bulging file folders.

He hadn't wanted to start issuing subpoenas yet; that would tip off too many other people. But now it looked like he had no choice.

If O'Connor wants to skip after we've got him served, that's a different matter. An international fugitive is at least good for some good press, especially when we have him on tape trying to bribe a Capitol cop. That leaves us a lever to work on him with, when he wants to come home, which most people do sooner or later.

He picked up the phone and buzzed the secretary. "Barbara, I'd like you to take one of the subpoenas the chairman signed yesterday and fill in the name of Gilbert O'Connor, 2306 Bluebird Lane, Fairfax, Virginia, on it. Then ask Sergeant Hanrahan to bring it in to me please."

When Hanrahan came in, Gibb was almost through with item #15 on the Day-Timer list, a letter to the lead attorney in the Justice department Criminal Division, updating him on the investigation. That had to be drafted carefully, since it was Gibb's working assumption that whatever he told the Justice Department went straight on to United General.

"We are continuing to pursue several leads which we think will be promising," he murmured into the dictating machine. "If these leads pan out, we expect to be ready to begin hearings by early next month."

No mention of subpoenas yet; and no mention of Gilbert O'Connor. Let them read that in the papers like everybody else.

"Phil, here's the subpoena." Hanrahan stood at his desk. He was back in his black Capitol Police uniform.

"George, we've gotta try and keep this guy O'Connor around," Gibb said, "and I don't think we can wait."

"Yessir."

"So I want you to take this out to Fairfax and serve it on him."

Hanrahan grimaced. But before he could object, Gibb went on. "Look, I know he's your old friend and classmate and all that. But this had to happen sooner or later, and I don't want to miss him. Have you been out to his house?"

"The new one?" He nodded. "Once, at a St. Joseph's alumni meeting. Last summer."

"Good, so you can get there without getting lost. I know this is unpleasant for you, George, but if it's any consolation, this is a good way to preserve your cover. Tell him this subpoena just came down this afternoon, and it's the first you knew about it. That's true enough."

"Yeah, I guess so." Hanrahan sighed. He turned to leave.

"Call me as soon as you serve him," Gibb said. "I'll probably still be here."

When Hanrahan was gone, Gibb turned back to the dictating machine, and Item #16. "Strike that last sentence," he said firmly. "Make it read, 'If these leads pan out, we expect to begin hearings soon.' And put yesterday's date on the letter."

two

An RCR doesn't get any fringe benefits: "This is a non-career, part-time position," the postmasters are careful to tell you when you start, and repeat every chance they get, so you don't forget your lowly status. No sick leave, no vacation, no paid holidays. Time and a half for overtime, and that's it.

But if there are no benefits, there are certain experiences that seem to come with the job, informally but almost universally. When I started out, most of them happened to me twice, as if, being an egghead intellectual, I needed repetition to get the proper effect.

Knocking down a mailbox is one. The second time that

29

happened, my back bumper caught and kicked over a whole row of them nailed to a board fence out on Ox Road. Fortunately nobody saw me, and I crept quietly away.

Breaking down is another. Not me, the car. In fact, that one was getting to be a habit until I put a new battery in the wagon. Once I had to walk a mile and a half just to find a phone, and the people at the tail end of Route 66 didn't get their mail that day til well after dark. Ferris got irate calls about that one for sure; but no problem, he just blamed it on the sub.

Then there's going into a ditch. It can happen anytime, but in slush or rain is the worst, not just because you go in deeper, but also because all the tow trucks around are usually busy as hell and it takes hours for them to get to you.

In this case, though, when it happened to me, I did get some benefit from the experience. That's because the ditch in question was at the foot of Jennifer's driveway.

It was just after Thanksgiving. The mail was heavy, and rain had been coming down hard all that day, and when I saw there was a cert in the parcel tray for Mahmood on Fox Run Shoals, I was tempted to just put the yellow notification slip in the box and not hazard the driveway. The Christmas mail rush was already underway, I was running behind, as usual, and wanted to get it over with.

But Ferris had been on my case about leaving notification slips and not going up to the door. People call in and bitch about that too, if they were home at the time. And this cert was an envelope from Iran, and the stamps with the picture of the Ayatollah intrigued me.

The Mahmoods were always getting mail from the Middle East, mostly from Lebanon, including Islamic newspapers printed in Arabic. These were full of muddy photos of hooded mobs marching with their fists raised, and what looked like advice columns headed by mug shots of some mullah and a sketch of an open book, presumably the Koran. They made me wish I could read Arabic.

Besides this, there were a number of intriguing features about Mrs. Mahmood herself. She was American, for one thing.

That became clear when they got some checkbooks, and I saw that her full name was listed as Jennifer Williams Mahmood.

Another came one day, shortly after I started last fall, when Merle nudged me and gestured toward the counter. There she was in line, holding two small parcels wrapped extra-securely, obviously meant to be sent overseas.

She was a study in incongruity. She wore a shapeless tan coat, with a big white scarf tied loosely around her head. This costume was becoming increasingly common in northern Virginia. But her voice, asking for stamps, gave no hint of an accent, and there was none of the confusion of the recent immigrant in her questions to Andy about postage and insurance. Her eyes were striking too, grey-green, and wisps of dark blond hair protruded from under the edge of the scarf. The two little boys hanging on to her coat seemed equally mismatched: they were blond, but with dark eyes and light olive skin.

The trio was wildly out of place in the line, bracketed by stylish suburban moms with designer sunglasses on one side and a couple of rednecks in puffy parkas and Caterpillar caps on the other.

"Married a freakin' A-rab," Merle muttered, and turned disdainfully back towards his case. I later learned that besides being racist, this was inaccurate, as Iranians are anxious to point out that they are not Arabs, but Persians. Whatever that means.

I stood there for another minute at least, though, a bundle of letters in my hand, fascinated.

She wasn't exactly beautiful, though what could you really tell in that dowdy getup? But there was something striking about those eyes, and I thought I saw an underlying melancholy in her expression, even when she smiled at Andy as she took her stamps. I couldn't stop looking even when she glanced past Andy and saw me staring.

three

Given her name, her appearance and her unique mix of mail, I was more than curious. When the weather was tolerable, I was always ready to pull on up their driveway with a cert or a parcel, just to see what I could see. And the incongruities multiplied from the first time I got to the top and stopped by their carport.

Beyond the house was a small horse stall, built by a previous owner. That was no surprise; this is a horsey neighborhood, full of nags you most often see being ridden by the preteen daughters of upward-striving families, wearing an approximation of English riding getup, and probably imagining themselves trotting alongside Princess Anne.

But the first time I saw the stall on a clear day, just after Columbus Day, I realized that the Mahmoods used it as a chicken coop. Half a dozen hens were clucking and pecking around it.

Then as I approached the door, there was an odd braying sound. Looking around, I saw they also had a goat on a chain.

Chickens and a goat. It was a good thing there were woods between them and the neighbors on either side. Horses were fine here, and maybe rabbits in hutches; but this was a little too Third World for South Fairfax tastes. For that matter, the line of shoes by the side door under the carport was a bit unusual too.

When my knock was answered by a dark woman wearing a dark red scarf who spoke no English, I was no longer surprised. I waved my cert at her and she went back inside, calling to someone. The room was bare except for a couple of mattresses shoved against the far wall. In the middle of the floor was a big metal pot, and next to it a pile of what looked like turnip greens.

The older of the two boys, about eight, came through the room. Again, that interesting contrast between the dark eyes and the light hair. Behind him, the other woman sat heavily down on the floor by the pot, picked up a handful of the greens, and began methodically tearing them into small pieces which she dropped into the pot, evidently resuming what she had been doing before I knocked.

I gave the boy the envelope; I didn't care who signed the slip and the return receipt, as long as I had them to bring back to Silas to get cleared of the damned things.

''Oh,'' he said brightly, ''This is from my school. See?''

I looked. Sure enough, the return address was for the

Greater Washington Islamic Academy. Why not, I reflected. The Washington wealthy of every other denomination had their private schools. "You on vacation?" I asked.

"Yes," he said, without an accent but enunciating crisply the way some bilingual people do. "For Columbus Day."

"Really?" I was surprised. "But you don't observe Columbus Day, do you?"

"No," he answered seriously, "we are Muslims. But it is the custom in America, so our teachers are having conferences."

Was there just a hint of resignation in his voice, an awareness of other impending American customs--Halloween and Christmas--also to be foregone? I couldn't tell.

"We go back tomorrow," he added, and sounded like he was anxious to get back. Stir crazy no doubt, out here in the woods and the only Muslim kids on the block. Probably no TV either, I was willing to bet, the tube being an endless blast of materialistic Christian propaganda. And how much fun can you have with a goat?

"Thank you, Hassan," said a voice behind him. It was Jennifer, coming through the room. Again, a shapeless dress and the scarf. Again, the grey-green eyes with the undertone of sadness in their expression. The boy obediently left the room.

She took the envelope. "You're not the regular carrier, are you?" she asked bluntly.

"Uh, no," I stumbled, "he transferred out a month ago, and it will be awhile before they get another regular assigned to the route. I'm a substitute, but I'll be delivering your mail for now."

She studied me a moment. "Tell me," she asked, "is it true that you will deliver stamps as well as mail?"

"Why, yes it is," I answered. I don't know if city carriers ever did, but rural carriers are still expected to be the post office on wheels for people on their routes, on the 1890 theory that country folks couldn't hitch up the team and drive their wagons into town every time they needed a stamp or a money order.

33

Out here in the burbs, though, few people knew of that tradition. Those who did drove me crazy, leaving envelopes in their boxes with dimes and pennies stacked on top that always went flying when I jerked open the door.

That's not to mention the time one lady left twenty two bucks in an envelope with just a note asking for 100 stamps, please, but no name or address. In my usual hurry, I threw it in my incoming mail tray, and of course when I got back to South Fairfax I couldn't remember where it came from. Naturally she called about it two days later very irate, but luckily for me Ferris was out and Silas gave me the message.

Now, however, it was suddenly a pleasure to affirm this custom. "Could you bring me eleven dollars worth?" Jennifer asked. I nodded, and she said, "Just a moment, I'll get the money," and walked silently back across the room. I could see she was barefooted. Pretty feet.

The woman with the red scarf was still sitting there, tearing up the greens, apparently oblivious to everything else.

Jennifer came back with a ten and a one. "You won't forget now, will you?" she said. Her tone was lower, and there was a hint of a smile on her face.

"Not a chance," I answered.

four

And verily, the next day I had no problem whatever remembering to put the fifty twenty-two cents stamps in an envelope with her address on it in the parcel tray, where I'd be sure not to miss them.

That afternoon was one of those days when it was almost fun being an RCR. The temperature was in the fifties; the sun was out, adding a touch of gold to the turning colors the trees and the dun grass. The mail was moderate, so I made good time. And best of all, the afternoon classical jock on WETA-FM was playing some of my favorite pieces on the PM show.

When I pulled up Jennifer's drive, window open on the passenger side and radio blasting, Herbert von Karajan and the Berlin Philharmonic were just winding up for the trio in the third

34

movement of Bizet's Symphony in C.

This was one of my all-time favorite passages. Besides that, it was amazing even to think that this bunch of lead-footed Teutons would tackle something as quintessentially Gallic as Bizet; so I couldn't bear to turn the radio off when I got to the carport, and left it and the motor running.

Jennifer answered the door and took the stamps and her mail, which included another one of the ominous-looking Arabic papers. She riffled through the bundle quickly, then looked up, not right at me but past my shoulder. "Is that Bizet?" she asked.

"Hey," I was surprised. "You got it. The Symphony. Von Karajan, can you believe it?"

Her eyes flicked briefly to me, then back again. She wasn't gazing at the car, I realized, but past it, into some middle distance where the music was coming back to her from another place or time.

"What a pity he never heard it performed," she said quietly. "How long was the manuscript lost--ninety years?"

"Try eighty," I said. This was liner note trivia, one of my specialties: "Wrote it in 1855, at the Paris Conservatory. It was discovered in their archives in 1935 by one of his biographers. Never been played til then. Too bad for the three generations that missed it. Bizet was seventeen when he wrote it, if you can believe that. You a fan of classical music?"

The eyes edged back to me. "I majored in music in college."

"Oh, really?" This was interesting. "Where?"

She lowered her gaze to the mail, and flipped through it again, a little nervously. "The first two years I was at Colorado State University--"

"You're kidding!" I interrupted. "I was at Laramie, just up the road, University of Wyoming."

Class of '68, distinguished among other reasons because we did not have a student strike that year. But that's another story, I thought; hell, it was another lifetime, in another universe. "Where after that?"

"Beirut. The American University there."

She saw my eyebrows go up; I couldn't help it. "It was

a peaceful place then," she added quietly.

That made me feel embarrassed. "No, I mean--" I fumbled, "a classical music major in Beirut?"

She shook her head, once more fingering the mail. "No, I switched to nursing there. It was better, and my husband--" Now she was fumbling.

Then she stepped back, inside the glassed-in screen door, and inside the invisible fence of her reserve. "Thank you for the stamps," she said as the door swung to, in the formal voice I remembered from when she spoke to Andy at the front counter.

"Right," I said, taking the hint. "If you need any more, just give us a call. We're in the book."

Then it was back to the wagon, where Herbert and company were making Bizet's finale sound like something fished up out of the Rhine.

She had shut the inside door before I was back in the driver's seat.

                                    five

Jennifer didn't call for more stamps. But there was a steady trickle of certs to deliver, as well as some insured parcels. Several of these were the beat-up foreign kind, tied up with prickly twine, some from Lebanon, others studded with Ayatollah stamps and green customs forms printed in French. Whenever I got to her driveway, I always made sure that the radio was on good and loud with whatever WETA was playing at the moment.

Unfortunately, the woman in the red scarf answered the door the next few times, and she had been briefed on signing the slips, which she did without a word. I saw Jennifer and the boys in Andy's line again once, but it wasn't until several deliveries later that I got to speak to anyone there again, when I brought another sizeable insured parcel.

It was right after Christmas, and the weather was warm, above fifty degrees that particular afternoon. WETA was playing Beethoven's Pastorale in celebration of the spring-like weather. I had the volume up very high for that one, old Ludwig's tourist sketches being the epitome of my romantic side.

36

Young Hassan was waiting when I got to the door. He opened it, heard the music, and wrinkled his nose.

"What's the matter?" I asked. "Don't you like Beethoven?"

A definitive shake of the head. His expression was solemn.

"So maybe you'd rather hear something, uh, Lebanese or Iranian?" I ventured.

Another shake. Then he grinned furtively. "Twisted Sister," he whispered. "Springsteen."

That was Jennifer's cue. "Hassan," she called from inside. "Your homework."

He called something foreign back to her, then left. She came and took the parcel, and signed the slip, being rather careful, it seemed to me, to pay no attention to the music. Her scarf had slipped back a little from her forehead, and I noticed that her hair was a dark strawberry blond, almost auburn. It looked thick and wavy, and very sexy concealed that way.

Seeing it made me unwilling to just walk away. "You don't like Beethoven either?" I asked when she handed me the slip and my ballpoint.

"It isn't that," she said. "You wouldn't understand."

"Try me. Or let me guess: For a Muslim it's a slippery slope--Beethoven leads to Twisted Sister, like they used to tell us marijuana leads to heroin."

Now she looked straight at me. "That's part of it," she admitted. "But mostly it's that it's all from a world that isn't his." She nodded in the direction Hassan had gone. "And can't be his."

"But why not?" I asked. "Aren't you American? Doesn't that make him an American too, even if you are Muslims?"

She smiled thinly. It was a nurse's professional smile, the kind you see when there's nothing much that can be done to help. She reached up and pulled her scarf down into place, covering up the bit of hair I had been ogling.

"Thank you," she said. Again the counter voice.

"Right," I said. "See you."

37

CHAPTER THREE

one

After that, it was red scarf every time for a couple weeks. 1985 started with a freeze, which thawed and was succeeded by several days of cold rain, alternating with just enough sleet to make driving dangerous. But what the hell, slippery roads meant slower driving and more time on the route. And more hours meant more money, which I needed.

On the last day of the rain, when the shoulders of all the roads on Route 66 were good and soggy, I ventured up the Mahmood driveway with another cert, this one from George Mason University.

Ah, George Mason, I thought, I know it well: Yet another Fairfax County institution growing fat fast on the apparently bottomless defense-related largess of the Reagan years. Also another place which wouldn't hire me. "We're full up with English instructors," the chairman said, with what he thought was an apologetic smile. "Perhaps a course or two in the spring; we'll let you know...."

Yeah, yeah.

Maybe if I could teach Arabic I would have been better off. At any rate, the cert was from the Languages Department, and my guess was that Jennifer's husband taught Arabic there. It was the logical thing.

The rain was pelting down as I pulled up under the carport, with Eugene Istomin just into the third movement of Schumann's Piano Concerto and giving it all he had. I huddled into my jacket and rapped on the door.

Jennifer answered, but didn't speak, reaching out both hands the way people do, taking the envelope with one and my proffered pen in the other. She scribbled quickly on the yellow slip, tore it off and handed it back.

As she did so the pen slipped from her fingers and rolled out beyond the edge of the carport, into the rain. "Sorry," she mumbled as I scrambled after it. By the time I straightened back up, the door was closed.

So to hell with you too, I thought, and got back in the car. The Schumann was rocking now, and it made me feel better at once. In fact, as I backed up I started to conduct it, the way I often do favorite pieces when nobody is watching.

The conducting was what sent me into the ditch. Halfway back down the incline of the drive, both hands waving in time with Istomin's fingers, the wagon started to veer off to the right.

I grabbed the wheel and hit the brake, but that was an overreaction: the back wheels fishtailed on the slick asphalt and before I knew it both tires on the right side were up to their rims in mud, with the rear wheel spinning and spraying muck but going nowhere except deeper in. Fox Run Shoals and the rest of Route 66 was only a few feet away, but I couldn't get there.

Istomin banged his way to a rousing climax and the music stopped. The jock came on, in his best carefully cultivated "natural" voice, quiet but earnest.

"Yes, that was truly a performance to get you up and moving," he enthused.

"Oh, shut up," I yelled, turning him and the engine off.

two

I sat there for a minute, as the rivulets zig-zagged down the windshield and drops drummed steadily on the roof. Then I got out, hunched down into my jacket again, and walked around the back of the car to see how bad it was.

It was bad. Stepping off the asphalt, my sneaker sank right through the grass into muck up to the eyelets. I jumped back and peered under the chassis. The right rear wheel was really in there, all right. The axle slanted at about a thirty degree angle.

I got back into the car and shook some of the water from

39

my hair. The wagon would have to be pulled out of this hole, no mistake. Christ, another case for Triple A.

But first, find a phone. Gotta call Ferris too, and tell him I'd be late. The Mahmood cert was the last one in the parcel tray, so at least I didn't have anything that had to get back to the office and be locked up. I wondered whether Jennifer had a phone, or if this was another item of western corruption she had forsworn. Or been forced to give up.

Jerk. Of course she had a phone. But who wanted to go back up there, and put up with any more of this silent treatment?

On the other hand, the next house was maybe a quarter mile away, in the rain.

Damn. There was no help for it. I got out and trudged up the drive to the door, getting good and wet, and knocked again.

Jennifer opened it only a couple inches. "Yes?"

"Hi. Uh--I'm stuck, I mean my car is stuck in your driveway, in the mud. It slid off. Could I use your phone to call for a tow truck?"

She hesitated, leaned out a few inches to peer down the drive at the car, while the rain ran down my neck, then said, "All right. Come in." I was surprised that she didn't tell me to take off my shoes.

The room was still bare except for the mattresses. Pale pastel blue paint on the walls, no pictures. It looked stark, out of place in this neighborhood. Two doors opened off it, one to a kitchen. Jennifer gestured in that direction. "The phone is in there."

The phone was on the wall inside the doorway. It had a long cord and I sat down at a small formica dinette and dialed.

Triple A's phone rang only once, then went into the "I'm sorry, all our lines are busy" recording routine, and treated me to a few minutes of elevator music.

Finally a woman came on. I told her I needed a tow and repeated my card number, which by now I knew by heart. She put me on hold again; more mindless music.

Then she was back, speaking very carefully. "I'm sorry, Mr. Adams, but your membership expired last month."

40

"What?" I grabbed at my wallet, fumbled for the card. She was right; the expiration date was the end of December. Christ.

"Well, can I write the driver a check?"

"I'm sorry, all membership renewals are processed by our main office in Falls Church. It's open nine to five weekdays, or you can do it by mail."

"Sure," I said, "I'll be right over, soon as I get out of the mud," and hung up.

So what now? I slipped the card back in the plastic pocket of my wallet, and sat there looking at it without seeing it. And I noticed three things.

The first thing was that there was only seven bucks in the wallet. Not enough to pay for a tow.

The next thing I noticed, flipping idly through the pockets, was that the Shell Oil card was still there. Most of my other cards had all been canceled for nonpayment months ago. But Shell, apparently a company run by optimists, was still relying on mere threats and intimidation. So maybe there was a Shell dealer who could tow me. Check the yellow pages.

I looked around the kitchen for a phone book. And then I noticed the third thing: the kitchen, and the house, were quiet. I could hear the rain beating on the carport, and trickling hollowly in a downspout. But inside, no sounds of kids; no TV or radio. Nothing.

I got up and walked out of the kitchen. Jennifer was at the door, staring out, with the opened letter in her left hand. Her shapeless blue-grey dress went perfectly with the frumpiness of the scarf. The only bright color in the room was a flash of green on the George Mason letterhead. "Excuse me," I said, "but do you have--?"

She had heard my conversation, and brushed past me into the kitchen. "The phone books are here," she said, pulling open a drawer. She seemed more preoccupied than brusque.

Finally a bit of luck. Eddie's Fairfax Shell answered on the first ring, and it was Eddie himself; and yes, they had a tow truck. Sure they'd send it out; I told them the address. "But we're awful busy, with the weather and all," said Eddie. "It'll be

41

awhile before we can get there.''

"How long?''

"Could be a couple hours. Gimme the number and I'll call you when we're on the way. Meantime, if I was you, I'd set back and watch me a soap opera or two.''

"Thanks. If I can find a TV.''

I dialed the station. Andy answered--Ferris was out, thank god. I left the message, hung up, and sat there a moment, taking in the kitchen.

It was clean and looked well-used, but was sparse by Route 66 standards. Some mismatched dishes were drying in a plastic drainer; next to the drain stood a portable microwave. Beside it was a small radio and cassette player, with a big antenna and short wave frequency markings on it. A few pots hung on nails on one wall, with not a copper bottom in the lot. It was the kind of place any self-respecting South Fairfax housewife would put at the top of her list of places to re-do.

I turned around. "I'm afraid it will be awhile,'' I started.

Jennifer nodded; she had her back to me, facing the door again. This time her forehead was touching the glass, and I could see a shine on her cheek. She was crying silently.

I stood up. "I'm sorry,'' I said. "I don't mean to intrude. I'll go wait in my car.''

She shook her head. "No.'' It was almost a whisper, and she was still facing the window. A silvery circle of mist had formed on the glass a few inches from her mouth.

"Don't. I don't want you to go.''

three

So I stood there, fumbling for words like a key lost in my overstuffed pants pockets. "Is--is something wrong?''

She turned away from the door. "Yes,'' she said, lifting the hand with the letter in it. "This. My husband just lost his job.'' She moved past me and sat in the chair opposite mine.

"Oh,'' I said, and sank back down. This was something I could relate to. "What happened?''

She put the letter carefully down on the table. "He's been

42

teaching Arabic and Mideast studies." So I had guessed at least half-right. "And they're not renewing his contract."

"That's tough." I was all sympathy, but felt unsure how well I could express it. It brought back a familiar hollow feeling in my gut to hear of this. "Why aren't they renewing him?"

"I don't know. It's all vague cliches." She picked up the letter and looked at it. "'With sincere regret,'" she read, "'the needs of the department', and of course 'budgetary constraints.' Et cetera."

I snorted. "Yeah, I think I know it by heart. Does it close 'With every good wish for your future'?"

She glanced up, showing me those grey-green eyes, now rimmed with red. She grinned a little, though grimly. "'With best wishes' actually, but that's pretty close. How do you know this so well?"

"Been through it. Over at Arlington Community. I was teaching English." I pulled myself up in mock-anger. "I mean, pardon me, madam, but do I look like a career mailman?"

She chuckled at that, in spite of herself. "It never occurred to me. Though come to think of it, you are the first postman I ever discussed music with."

"Well, I'm just doing the mail until I can find another teaching gig."

"You mean," she said, knowing the score well enough, "you expect to be doing it for awhile."

"Yeah," I admitted. "Who'm I kidding? And what about you? What are you and your husband going to do now?"

four

It was the wrong thing to say. Hearing about my troubles had diverted her momentarily. Now, remembering, she sank back into the sadness, and her eyes began to fill again. "He'll want us to go home," she said, again in a near-whisper. "To Beirut. That's where his family lives. It's where he is now."

"And do I gather you're not too keen on the idea?"

Another thin, rueful grin. "Right. Except--except, then again maybe it is the best thing to do. I don't know."

43

"Well, I can understand your reluctance," I said. "From what I hear Beirut's not a very safe city these days, especially for Americans. But on the other hand, if you're going to go back, you better go soon, or there may not be anything left to go back to."

"There will always be something to go back to," her tone was defiant. "There is more to Lebanon than fighting and what the Western press sees. Though you're right, it isn't always a safe place." A sigh. "But that's not what bothers me most about going back. I'm a nurse; blood doesn't frighten me."

"What does?"

She looked up with a questioning expression for a moment, as if asking herself how far to trust this damp stranger in her kitchen. Apparently she decided to push a little further: "Leaving here," she whispered. "Leaving the states."

That surprised me. "But I would think a good Muslim would be happy to get out of the U.S. With our decadence and corruption; the Great Satan and all that. What about your kids? You seem to work pretty hard at keeping them away from all this, but you must know it's an uphill climb, even with a Muslim school. Especially in Fairfax County. I think they invented consumerism here."

She nodded. "I know. But the problem is, I'm an American. And even though I hate all this, I like it too. Besides, it's only at Rashid's insistence that the boys go to the Muslim Academy. Still, they're not the main reason."

"Which is--?"

She looked up sharply now, and a fierceness came into her voice. "It's me. It's what it would mean for me. As a woman, I mean."

I considered this a moment. "You mean veils and harems and such? But I would think you were used to that. I mean, from the way you dress." This felt awkward, but there it was.

In any case, she was shaking her head slowly, reflectively. "There's no harem," she said, "and the veil as you call it is the least of my problems. In any case this is not much of a veil, and all that is in a state of flux there these days, like everything else. But some things are more deeply rooted, and

44

harder to get away from.'' She trailed off, her gaze now inward, seeing something in memory.

"Like what?'' I persisted, a little more sharply than I'd intended. But, damn it, I thought, if we're going to talk about this, let's talk about what we're talking about.

It brought her up short. She suddenly focussed in on me, as if she had been carrying on a monologue and I had just appeared out of nowhere.

"You know,'' she said quietly, "back home--in Beirut, I mean--a conversation like this would be completely unheard of. Scandalous. A married woman talking alone in her house with a strange man. And an infidel too.''

I sighed and started to get up. "Well,'' I grunted, "I've been called a lot of names, but infidel is a new one. Look, I don't mean any trouble. If you want me to wait in my car, I'll-''

"No.'' She reached out and put one hand lightly on my damp sleeve. I glanced down: slim but not delicate fingers, unmanicured, and a sensible digital wrist watch with a black plastic strap. Nice skin color.

I sat back. She surveyed me again for a long moment. Then she drew a silent but apparently decisive deep breath and said, "It's my mother-in-law. Rashid's mother.''

I rolled my eyes and let out a sardonic groan. "So old-lady trouble is a crosscultural and ecumenical hassle, is it?''

Another shake of the scarf. "You don't have any idea, really. It's not like here at all. In traditional Arab culture, the mother-in-law is the real ruler inside the family. She controls the money, the food, everything. Even after a son is married; she lives with him, or he with her, unless the son can find a good excuse to get far enough away....''

"And you just lost your excuse.''

"Right.''

"But if you'll pardon my asking, how did a nice American girl like you get tied up with a guy and a mother-in-law like that?''

Now she leaned back in the small chair and her gaze wandered to the ceiling. "Oh,'' she said, "it was easier than you might think.''

45

"I was raised over there," she went on, "in Saudi Arabia and Iran. My father worked for Aramco, not drilling oil, but more like an in-house academic, teaching languages and culture to the American employees. His parents were Presbyterian missionaries in Palestine, and he grew up there."

She wiped at one eye. No makeup smear, I noticed. "We always lived outside the American compounds, in Riyadh and Teheran. As a kid I learned Arabic almost as soon as English; I sort of breathed in Islam the way you breathe in air pollution here."

"But what about your old man? How did a Presbyterian missionary's son take to having a Muslim daughter?"

She shrugged. "Oh, he had left the Presbyterian part behind long ago. My folks are retired now, they live near Philadelphia. But their hearts are still in the Middle East, and I think he was almost pleased about me. Going native, he calls it. And it didn't really happen until I came to Colorado for college."

"You converted to Islam in Colorado?"

Now she laughed. "Well, what happened is that I met Rashid there. He was doing graduate work in English and was planning to go back to Teheran afterward. When we decided to get married, he explained that he couldn't bring home a wife, especially not one he had chosen himself, and most especially not an American, unless she was also a Muslim."

"You mean, 'Look, dad, it's not like you're losing a son, Muhammad is gaining a convert?'"

"More or less. Except it wasn't dad's reaction that counted; it was mom's. And like I said, back in Iran the veil was the easy part compared to dealing with her. By the time the revolution came, Rashid's father had died, and the rest of the family left for Lebanon when Khomeini's tyranny became clear."

"Wait a minute," I said. "If Rashid's family is so all-fired Muslim, why didn't they like the Ayatollah?"

She sighed. "You really don't know anything about it, do you? Hardly anyone here does." She collected herself. "Khomeini represents Islam about as much as--as the Ku Klux

46

Klan and its burning crosses represent Christianity. He doesn't even speak for most of the Shia'"

I shrugged. "Whatever you say. But am I right that politics wasn't really the biggest problem for you?"

Her voice dropped again. "No. of course not. Governments come and go, the matriarchy remains. It got worse after we went to Beirut. Fatima was old, she was alone, really, and away from home. She dealt with it by hanging on to her son, and his sons, tighter and tighter, going back to traditional attitudes I thought I'd seen the last of. And Rashid fell into line; he didn't like it, at one level, but his part in the play was bred into him too. Before long I was an outsider in my own home. It's an old story in Islamic culture."

"Sounds awful. How did you get away?"

She sniffed. "I'm still an American, you know. I have rights--and I had my passport, enough savings for a plane ticket to New York, and an aunt there who had said I could always land on her doorstep. So I told Rashid that the boys and I were leaving, with him or without...."

"So he came."

"He was relieved, actually. He has two brothers, one in the states and the other in Lebanon who is widowed, and that one seemed content to have his mother move in and run his life. And Rashid knew there wasn't any future for him in Beirut. He was political--who wasn't?--but against all the terrorism and militancy. Always."

She stiffened, in remembered, proud defiance. "He was even ready to recognize Israel, if that could mean getting a Palestinian state someday, though he knew better than to say so in public. We came to the states three years ago. And it was working. Mostly."

six

I began to wonder how much more intimate her tale was going to get. The more she talked, the more it seemed to spill out: Rashid's seeming success in making the transition to teaching Arabic to English speakers instead of vice versa. His

47

continuing anxiety over his mother, caught in Lebanon's endless slide into chaos, as well as worry over the unhappy fate of his Iranian homeland, and the whole boiling pot of the Middle East.

Then his brother's illness, which prompted a return visit over the Christmas holidays--a visit prolonged by both his brother's failure to get better and some moonlighting teaching English at the American University in Beirut. But the trip had lasted too long for George Mason, it turned out.

I needed a breather. "Do you mind if I turn on the radio, down low?"

She shook her head. I reached over and flipped the switch on the shortwave. It was set--I should have known--on WETA. The jock, still talking smooth as fabric softener, was just announcing some Strauss waltzes, to be done in the grand style by Karl Bohm and the Vienna Philharmonic. I kept it low, and turned back to her.

"I wonder what you mean, it was working for you here? In the States, that is--don't you feel like a sore thumb, or a fish out of water?"

"Not really," she said easily. "Actually, being Muslim has a lot of advantages here. The scarf looks dowdy to you, I suppose; but it keeps the sexists at bay. And because this isn't Iran, I can work and do the things I want to do. So I get some of the best of both worlds."

"Okay, I can see how that's good for you. And Rashid?"

"He likes it, too, I think. At least he did. Without a teaching job, I don't know."

I couldn't resist trying for another laugh. "He could always drive a cab out of National Airport," I said. "It's easier than delivering mail, because he wouldn't have to know his way around; none of the rest of them do."

It worked. She giggled again, not only not minding my sarcasm, but seeming to grab onto it. "You know," she murmured, "I think you're cheering me up."

Out of the other ear, I heard Karl's Vienna boys just launching into the intro of the Blue Danube.

An impulse struck me; what the hell? I stood up stiffly,

bowed, then opened my arms. "Madam," I announced, "I have only just begun to cheer you up. For my next effort, may I have this waltz?"

seven

She recoiled in what I saw was only mock horror. "Waltz?" she asked. "Do I even remember how?"

"If you don't, I will instruct you. And--" I bent down to pull off one of my damp sneakers, and hopped on one foot while tugging at the other one-- "I promise I will not step on milady's delicate feet."

Then I paused. "But if I'm stepping out of line--"

"Of course you are," she said, grinning. "You have absolutely no business being here, no business getting me to tell you all about myself, and no business asking me to dance. In Beirut I would be in deep trouble."

She hesitated, frowning at the envelope on the table between us. Then she pushed it away from her. "But in Fairfax, I will be glad to try a waltz. I think I need it."

She stood up. I extended my arms, and she came tentatively toward me, putting one hand lightly on my shoulder, and barely touching my fingertips with the other. We moved awkwardly into the step, and had not gone more than three bars or so when she hit one of the kitchen chairs, knocked it over and lost her balance.

I grabbed her around the waist, steadied her and stepped right back into the rhythm.

I'm not a great dancer, but I was good enough for this. And the fall was the end of our sixteen-inches-for-Muhammad posture. She moved more and more easily, and as the Danube built to its crescendo her scarf and then her cheek brushed mine. I felt her breasts press glancingly against my chest.

When the music died away she stepped back, smiling and looking a little flushed, to catch her breath.

"How long," I asked quietly, "has it been since you did that?"

"A long time," she whispered. "A very long time."

49

Another minute of standing there, and the spell would be broken; I could feel it, and didn't want it to go.   There were pushbuttons on top of the radio. I took a chance, reached around and punched the middle one.

What a stroke of luck--the oldies station. Her secret vice revealed. Even better, it was Roberta Flack, just getting started with ''Killing Me Softly.'' I beckoned gently to Jennifer. ''One more?'' I asked.

She came to me, and this time not in an upright waltz posture, but closer and yielding.

Now it was slow-number-at-the-high-school-dance time all over again; her forehead against my chin, the curves of her pressing gently into me. I hunched over a little, sliding my cheek down the edge of the rough scarf to meet hers, moving in slow circles.

This being ''Twofer Thursday,'' they segued from ''Killing Me Softly'' right into''The First Time.''

eight

Before it ended she wasn't dancing anymore, she was clinging to me.   Something had been stirred awake in her, something both vulnerable and fierce. I heard her breath catch and pulled back enough to look at her.

She was crying again. ''No,'' she whispered, ''don't look at me. And don't stop holding me.'' I closed in again and took a step, but she didn't follow.

When I paused, her hand slipped from mine and moved to my face, pulling it around and down to hers. Her lips were wet with the tears, but they thrust against mine without hesitation. The saltiness was brief and exciting.

Roberta Flack faded, and there came, in a tingle of electric triangles, Cat Stevens and his sweet-sad ''Oh Very Young.''   The lyrics didn't really apply to me anymore, or to Jennifer either; but maybe you had to be a formerly very young person to really get the message.

And, I found myself half-remembering, didn't Cat Stevens give it all up to become an orthodox Muslim? I seemed to recall

50

something in a supermarket tabloid, a muddy picture of a hooded figure, and friendly comments about the Ayatollah....

Funny how your mind can wander even in the clinches. But Jennifer didn't let that continue long. Her kiss was hungry and open, and my reflexes took over. If her husband had been gone for two months, it had been most of a year since Sally the Salacious Sophomore had last welcomed me into her bed.

My right hand groped up Jennifer's back til the fingers closed on the edge of her scarf, and pulled. It slid off, and I opened my eyes. Her hair was pulled back into a short, thick braid.

The sight of it aroused me, as if I had never seen a woman's hair before. I pulled away slightly to admire it, stroking first the thick strands and then her face.

She looked back at me, eyes only half-open, then leaned in for another probing kiss. In a moment she moved her lips to my ear. "Come with me," she murmured.

"What about the boys?" I whispered. "And the other woman?"

"You're in luck. They've all gone to Williamsburg, on a history field trip. Won't be back til tonight."

She turned and extended one hand. I took it and followed her through the door on the other side of the kitchen, past a bathroom and into a large bedroom. There was a bookshelf partition on the far side of a double bed, behind which sat a desk and typewriter, a cramped mini-office.

Jennifer wasted no time. She pulled the tail of my shirt out of my pants, unbuttoned the first few buttons, then reached behind her back to the zipper of her dress. I stopped her. "Wait," I said. "First, your hair."

There was something unfathomably exotic in her half-smile. "Of course," she answered, and pulled the braid apart expertly, shaking it loose.

What can I say? The sight of her unrestrained dark blonde mane excited me more than anything else. Not that I had much time to think about it. In a minute her dress was on the floor, with my shirt and pants in a heap nearby, and we were on the bed.

51

It was more than an hour later before she let up, giving a last cry of climax and collapsing beside me, clumps of the hair now sticking sweatily to her cheek. "You're really something," I said, amazed and exhausted.

She giggled. "Does it surprise you that a Muslim woman could be passionate?"

"I guess so," I admitted.

"More Western ignorance," she said, kissing me. "It is a religious duty for a Muslim woman to get satisfaction from sex."

"In that case," I said, "Allah be praised."

She started to grin at me, but then stopped, as if my wisecrack had reminded her of something. "Oh, the time," she said, and slid off the bed. "I'll be right back."

She slipped out the door, and in a moment I heard splashes from the bathroom. Then she was back, signaling me to wait as she passed behind the bookshelf partition.

I sat up quietly, wondering what the hell was going on. Then I noticed a mirror on top of a dresser by the bedroom door. If I moved a little to my left, it reflected the desk, and Jennifer moving before it.

I watched fascinated as she bent down to unroll something, then knelt and bowed forward, away from the mirror. The curve of her naked back was long and graceful in that position, and I could hear her murmuring something. In a few moments she rose, rolled up what I guessed was her prayer rug, and then came back to the bed.

She sat down, saw my gaping expression, and laughed. "What's the matter with you?" she said. "You look like you saw a ghost."

I didn't know where to start. "Were you doing what I think you were doing?"

"You mean praying?" she said. "Sure. It was time."

I was nonplussed. "But is it really--I mean...." I trailed off.

She raised an eyebrow. "You mean, how can a religious

woman get out of an adulterous bed and go directly to the worship of God?''

Her directness was breathtaking. I exhaled sharply. ''Well, yes, I guess that is what I was wondering. I mean, I'm in no position to moralize or anything. But it seems, I don't know, incongruous.'' To say the least, I thought.

She shook her head. ''I don't expect you to understand,'' she said, pulling the sheet to her waist. ''But remember, Allah sees everything, and knows what's going to happen anyway. So what am I hiding from Him? And the classic Muslim prayers begin, 'In the Name of Allah, the Compassionate, the Merciful.' That's the God I was praying to. Not some Ayatollah. That's a fanatic stereotype, which is promoted by the western media. Rashid fought it in Iran, and we fight it still, in Lebanon and here too.''

''But I'll bet Rashid wouldn't approve of this as a way of fighting stereotypes,'' I said.

She moved over and kissed me. ''You're right. But if Allah has to know about it, Rashid doesn't.'' She sat back against the pillows, and let out a contented sigh. ''And I feel so much better now, that we're not going to tell him. He has enough to worry about.'' She reached up and traced one finger down my cheek. ''You really do cheer me up, Perry. Very much.''

I thought I saw a hint of the old melancholy returning to her eyes, and was just bending down to kiss her again, when the phone rang in the kitchen.

We both jumped. She got up, reached into a closet by the dresser for a bathrobe, and left. I heard her answer the phone, listen, then tell the caller to wait.

Her head appeared in the doorway. She was brushing her hair, which looked thick and luscious. ''It's Eddie,'' she said. ''For you.''

''Eddie?'' I asked, disoriented. Did I know an Eddie?

''Eddie's Fairfax Shell,'' she reminded me. ''Your tow. The mail must go through, remember? And the boys will be home pretty soon anyway.''

''The truck'll be there in about five minutes,'' Eddie said when I got to the phone, adding, ''sorry for the delay. But you know how it is, days like this.''

"Yeah, yeah," I replied mechanically.

But I was thinking that he hadn't delayed nearly long enough for my taste. Besides which, I did not know how it was on days like this. Not days like this, not at all.

For that matter, I thought, I've never been particularly religious. But after this afternoon, be it Allah or Jesus, there must be a God somewhere.

CHAPTER FOUR

one

The image of Mr. O'Connor falling into the shattered glass of his door was still there in my vision as I pulled up to Jennifer's carport. The shooter may have missed me, but I was still shaking. I rubbed the knot on my head. And I could see right away that no one was home.

Shit. Where are they when you need 'em? Of course, we hadn't actually had a date. We never did, really. I'd just bring the certs, hand them over with an inquiring look, and when she gave me back the slips she'd whisper, "Tomorrow," or "Come back at four," or even, "This week is no good," and off I'd go. If I was coming back, I'd pull my car up behind the pony stall, away from enquiring eyes.

But bullets on Bluebird Lane had rather decisively shifted my attention away from the prospects for sex, into a strictly survival-oriented mode. Now I was interested in cover, in case whoever had that gun was coming after me.

I turned around in the carport, then crept back down the sloping drive. Braking a few feet back from the entrance, I slumped down to where I could just see over the wheel, minimizing my profile while keeping an eye on the road and approaching cars.

Traffic was light. In ten minutes I saw three station wagons, an electrician's van, an old Sentra bearing a Domino's Pizza roof sign, and two otherwise unidentifiable sedans.

Under this unremitting assault of suburban normality, my paranoia receded somewhat, and then I began to feel tired; a touch of shock, I think.

I should be safe here, I reckoned, behind the screen of trees along the road. Leaning back, I let my eyes close, and felt my breathing slowing. Just relax a minute.

The familiar putt-putting sound of Merle's postal jeep speeding by, on the way back from his route, woke me up with a start. The shadows had moved twenty or thirty degrees toward the east. I was still alive.

I was also still technically at work. The jeep noise reminded me that a tray of undelivered mail was sitting in the back of the wagon. And the mail must go through.

Would the shooter be lurking nearby, waiting patiently to clip me right by somebody's box? And shouldn't I drive to the nearest phone and report what looked like murder, plus attempted murder? And, oh yes, the loss of the yellow slips for O'Connor's reds?

Now I was getting scared again--not only of the killer, but also of the Postal Inspection Service, the FBI, and the various other kinds of cops who would probably want a piece of this action, and a bite out of my behind. Would anybody believe my story?

I rubbed my head again, and decided on a middle course. About a mile down Fox Run Shoals there was a country store, Ferris's. It was a throwback to an earlier time, stubbornly preserving a sense of authentic rurality just a stone's throw from the suburban developments that were eating up the woods all around it.

Ferris's had three old gas pumps topped with milky glass lollipops outside, a small lunch counter inside, big checkerboard sacks of kibbled chow for pets and livestock stacked along the far wall, and a row of rental trailers in a muddy lot out back. Jennifer bought food for the goat and chickens there, and I stopped in now and then for a soda and a cup full of their splendidly fat and greasy western fries, well-doused with Frank's Original Red Hot sauce.

But more important to me now, Ferris's also had a pay phone, inside and out of the line of sight of anybody nearby with an Uzi or a Luger or whatever the hell it was.

I started the car and pulled out onto the road. I turned on the radio.

56

The news was on: The Space Shuttle was almost ready for its celebrity crew of a New Hampshire teacher. There had been more gunplay in Beirut, another attempted kidnapping of an American diplomat. But no mention of murder in South Fairfax. I turned it off.

A dozen stops later, with Ferris's in sight, I reflexively checked the rear view mirror as I started to pull away from a box.

Red lights were flashing on a cruiser pulling up behind me.

two

Lorena at the front desk smiled uncertainly at the old man, revealing a shiny set of braces, and said, "Um, just a minute, sir." She stood up and sidled quickly back past the partition into the AA's portion of the cramped congressional office.

Sue Lee, the Administrative Assistant, was tall, with delicate features, long straight Gloria Steinem hair, large glasses and a no-nonsense demeanor. She stood by her desk, at eye-level with a sepia portrait of a sad-eyed Robert E. Lee framed in dull gold. Many constituent visitors inferred from this that she was a descendant of the Old Dominion's warrior patron saint. She was not, in fact, but did nothing to discourage the assumption.

With a studied drawl and a hand of iron, she ruled the staff of United States Representative Richard Abernathy, Fifth District of Virginia. Rumor had it that she likewise ruled the Congressman with equal, though carefully camouflaged, authority. She did nothing to quash that gossip either.

On one corner of her cluttered desk a small television screen glowed with the closed circuit image of another Congressman, declaiming fervently but soundlessly to a large C-SPAN audience and a near-empty House chamber.

"Sue?" Lorena asked timidly.

Her boss peered up sidelong from a memo in her hand, a phone cradled under one ear. Her eyebrows rose inquiringly.

"Sue," Lorena repeated in a whisper, "he's back. That guy who talks funny. This is the third time today."

57

Part of Sue Lee's job, a minor part, was deflecting the steady stream of off-the wall visitors who circulated through the corridors of power like cockroaches in a nighttime kitchen. The cops kept the visibly disheveled and the audibly ranting outside, so those who got past them looked normal, neatly dressed and soft-spoken.

But along with their polite smiles they also carried with them, or so Sue and her colleagues had on various occasions been earnestly assured, the definitive plan for world peace through universal colonic irrigation; transcripts of interviews with their angelic UFO abductors; or proof that, rather than three gunmen on the Grassy Knoll, there had in fact been ten, and all had been tenors in the Mormon Tabernacle Choir.

Yes, they nodded when Sue feigned astonishment, it did sound incredible, but it was all true. Furthermore, they had the documentation right here, in small, crowded type on muddy xerox copies drawn from battered briefcases. That is, unless the CIA-- which was trying to control their minds with hidden radios--had stolen or tampered with the documents again.

These visitors were usually harmless, and some were even constituents, it being only a three-hour drive from the District. So getting rid of them had to be done with tact.

But it had to be done.

Normally the task was delegated to the interns and receptionists. It was part of the stern winnowing by which Sue Lee gauged which of these callow youth were of the rugged stock that could bear up under the weight of carrying on the People's Business. Many were called; few were chosen.

Sue briefly studied Lorena's anxious face. She was not at all sure the younger woman had what it took.

"Just a minute," Sue said into the phone. The memo dropped to her desk and she placed a palm over the phone's mouthpiece. "Is he bothering you?" she mouthed to Lorena.

"Not really," the younger woman whispered back. "He just keeps coming. And he talks funny. Calls me 'thee' and 'thou.'"

At this information, Sue nodded knowingly. "An older man?" she whispered. "Kind of stooped? A bit shabby?"

58

Lorena showed silver again. "Yeah. That's him. Has he been here before? Is he some kind of Amishman or something?"

Sue shook her head, then uncovered the phone. "Lemme call you back in a minute, Fred. No, I won't forget you. Listen, I know it's important." She hung up, and murmured, "Everything's important, right?" then motioned for Lorena to follow her back to the front desk.

To Lorena's surprise, Sue walked right up to the old man. He was sitting by the front door, under a mural-size color photo of a Blue Ridge mountain vista.

Sue shook his hand. "Mr. Penn," she said, "Good to see you again."

"Thank thee, Sue," Penn said, rising, "the pleasure is always mine. Though today I was hoping to speak with Richard briefly. I have some documents to share with him about the planned prison in Martindale."

The AA checked the wall clock by Lorena's desk, just above the phone console, on which several lights were blinking. "Well," she hedged, "normally I'd take you right in for a minute, but he's got Mr. Gibb in with him now. They're working on some important Gov. Ops. Committee business, and he said they couldn't be disturbed."

She glanced at the clock again. "There's supposed to be a floor vote in about half an hour, though. If you want to wait, you could probably walk over to the House chamber with him when he goes to vote."

A phone buzzed behind the partition. Glancing back at the console, Sue saw a light blinking at the bottom of its column. "Lorena," she said over her shoulder, "that's my inside line. Could you grab it for me, please?"

"Sure." Lorena vanished.

"--I'm not sure I can wait that long today," Penn was saying. "But perhaps tomorrow--?"

"Let me check his schedule," Sue said smoothly, reaching for a big appointment book that lay open on Lorena's desk. "Hmmmm, it's pretty full, as usual--" She scanned a page. "But you've got time, Mr. Penn. I see that the markup on that bill has been put off, for a week or two--"

59

A gasp that was almost a shriek came from behind the partition.

"Sue!" Lorena shouted. "It's Sergeant Hanrahan. He says he's found somebody murdered out in South Fairfax, a Mr. O'Connor, and he has to tell Phil Gibb right--"

She rushed to the front desk, her eyes wide, braces glinting, and faltered when she saw Penn eyeing her with obvious interest. Should he be hearing all this?

But Sue gave her no time to fret. "Hold the calls," she snapped crisply. She scribbled rapidly on a memo sheet. "I'm going in." Then to Penn, "Excuse me. I think this is an emergency." She folded the memo as she hurried past her cubicle to the big oak door. She tapped firmly twice, and let herself in.

Behind her, the visitor again sat down under the photo mural, appearing thoughtful as Lorena feverishly punched at the blinking buttons.

When she finally caught up and paused for breath, she looked up and saw he was still sitting there. He said quietly, "Friend, I wonder if thee'd let me use a telephone for a moment, if one is free?"

three

RCR's don't make much, I thought. But a postmaster's pay, however much more, isn't worth it.

By this time of the afternoon, Ferris's expression had sunk past harried to downright haggard. Half-moons sagged under his eyes and his desk ashtray was full of mangled cigarette butts. He'd been juggling paperwork, customer complaints, and delivery hassles for eight hours, and there was no end in sight. Whatever his salary, I figured, it wasn't enough.

By contrast, the dark-suited, unsmiling man seated next to him seemed ominously fresh, ready for action, as if he might leap from his seat and do forty pushups, or maybe break both our necks with a pair of precise karate chops. In his right hand was a silver barreled pen, poised over a small black notebook lying open on the edge of Ferris's desk.

60

I sensed what he was before Ferris spoke. "Adams, this is Inspector Harper."

Another cop.

Officer Cody of the Fairfax County Police had just dropped me outside the building. I had felt relieved when Cody first pulled up behind me on Fox Run Shoals; there was safety in a police escort. But by the time he finished asking me questions, it was clear he suspected me of being the shooter, and I felt lucky not to be under arrest and headed for the new highrise jail in downtown Fairfax City.

I had watched Cody in my rearview, talking into his microphone as we cruised slowly back to the station. I figured his people were briefed on my story, and wondered now if they had called Ferris and Harper.

They had.

"Mr Adams," Harper said without preamble, "do you have the 4936 for the registered mail you took out today?"

I shook my head. "Look, it--"

"I know," he said, raising the hand with the silver pen to stop me. His fingers were long and sinewy. "That question was really just a formality. We've been briefed about the killing of Mr. O'Connor. That could be, um, a mitigating circumstance."

That was comforting to know, I thought. I noted that he pronounced O'Connor as "O'Connuh." I figured it to be a New England accent.

"But strictly speaking," he was saying, "the murder is not our case. The Inspection Service preserves the sanctity of the mail, protects valuables that are sent through it, and investigates reported mail thefts."

The man talked like a textbook, and I didn't like the faint stress he put on "reported." He consulted some writing in the notebook. "It looks now," he went on, "as if those parcels contained a very large sum of currency and negotiable securities. We're not sure of the exact amount yet, but it's probably in the six to seven figure range. So having them accounted for is very important. A theft on that scale is a major felony."

He paused and looked up at me expectantly, as if I was

supposed to pull the yellow slip from behind my ear, or at least say something intelligent.

Seven figures. Major felony. I felt witless and inarticulate.

Finally I shrugged and mumbled, "Oh. That's a lot of money."

Ferris frowned and tapped a cigarette from a nearly empty pack. "I don't think you understand, Adams," he growled. "Until we have either those parcels or the signed 4936, we're liable for that money. Didn't Silas explain all this to you?" He blew smoke in my direction.

I shrugged again and nodded, hating the smoke and feeling hollow in the stomach. Perhaps I'd get to a downtown highrise cell yet.

Harper had a pencil mustache and big ears. His face creased into a tight, unconvincing, I'm-only-here-to-help-you smirk. "Of course," he said, "you haven't been charged with anything at this point."

He said it "chahhged". "--We'll be checking your story of what happened. In the meantime..." he trailed off and looked significantly at Ferris.

It was a cue. Ferris pulled the cigarette from his mouth. "In the meantime, Adams," he repeated, "You're suspended until further notice." He sighed. "It's a precaution I have to take."

"And we'd like to have you make a written statement, if you would," Harper picked up again smoothly. "I'd like to do that now, if you're ready."

Finally words came to me, with indignation. "Wait a minute," I said. "Don't I get to talk to a lawyer about this first, if I'm going to be giving statements in what could be a possible criminal case against me?"

Harper suddenly looked a bit uncomfortable. "Well, yes," he conceded. "You certainly have that right, and we could get back to you on that, if you prefer." He reached into his coat pocket, and handed me a card. "Go ahead and talk to your attorney. And that's my number. Call anytime, the sooner the better."

It was "numbah", "soonah," and "bettuh" coming from

62

his mouth.

"Sure," I said sarcastically.

My attorney? The last attorney I dealt with was a Legal Aid type who went over the papers for my divorce. He probably didn't remember my name; I wasn't sure I remembered his. I stuck the card in my pocket. "Am I right that I'm not under arrest now?"

Harper gave a grudging nod.

"So I can walk out of here if I want, right?" Now I was glaring at Ferris. "And if I don't have a job anymore, I don't need to stay here, right?"

Ferris's frown deepened. "I didn't say you were fired," he rumbled. "Just til we get this--"

There was a knock on the outside door, but I was out of the office, heading for my case, to pick up my lunch stuff and get the hell out of there.

Merle was waiting for me. He hadn't heard the office colloquy, and he was grinning. "Ah'll be goddammed if you haven't livened this old place up," he said. "What'll you think of next?"

"I need to think up a new job," I snapped. "And personally, I don't think it's so funny."

Merle sobered and turned toward the back door. "Come on," he called, "let's get a pizza and you can tell me about it."

"Sure," I mumbled. "Just don't ask me for my goddam numbah."

"Say what?" Merle called.

"Never mind."

four

"Did thee really need to suspend that young man, Adams?" Lemuel Penn asked.

Walter Ferris slumped in his worn metal armchair. "I don't know," he said. "I suppose so. The Inspector was expecting me to take some kind of action."

"He did seem somewhat, er, officious," Penn agreed. "But does thee really think Adams stole that money, or killed that man O'Connor?"

63

Ferris was silent a moment. He rubbed a tobacco-stained finger along the frame of the photo of the woman holding the child. The snow drops, wedged into a corner of the brass, looked stiff and brittle, as if they were cut from onionskin paper.

"You mean," he said finally, "do I suspect him?" He shook his head. "Not really. If he had done it, why the hell would he come back here? He would've cleared out, driven straight to Dulles and been on the first plane to anywhere over the border. That's what I would have done."

Ferris shifted in his chair. "The thing is, Lem, it's not just Adams who's in trouble. I'm under suspicion too. Not the prime suspect, but I'm on the list. With maybe a million bucks gone, Harper can't rule anything out: He could figure I was in cahoots with Adams, figuring to split the cash later. It's happened."

"A million?" Penn's dark eyebrows climbed his wrinkled forehead. "That much?"

"Maybe a bit less, according to Harper. They're still checking. Anyway, even if they don't think I was in on it, it's still my responsibility. The office is like a ship, I'm the captain. The missing parcels were in my office safe overnight. I signed for them."

He picked up a sheaf of blank forms, headed, "Incident Report."

"If the money isn't found, there will be piles of reports like this going all the way to Headquarters, and my name will be in all of them, looking bad. At best it'll be the end of my career."

He crumpled the papers. "I could fight it, of course. The postmaster's league is good at that.

He sighed. "But you ever seen what that does to people? They get obsessed. Worn down, hollow-eyed. They often win, eventually--that is, if they don't have a stroke first."

Ferris tossed the wad of paper at a wastebasket in the corner. It bounced off the rim onto the floor. He ignored it and stabbed at Penn with the lighted cigarette. "I don't want it to end like that, Lem." He slumped back again, and gazed toward the ceiling of the small, untidy office.

64

"That's why I asked you to come back over when you called." He cleared his throat and his expression became combative. "Look, this job is a grind most of the time, but it's also real work. People need their mail. Half a billion pieces, that's what the Postal Service handles every day."

He rubbed his sagging face. "A hundred thousand pieces or so come in right here every morning. People don't think about it much, except to complain. But mail keeps this town going. Keeps the damn country going. And I've been getting the mail to almost five thousand homes and businesses in South Fairfax, six days a week, for a lot of years."

He raised a fist and thumped it weakly on the desk as he added, "More or less on time, too."

An empty coffee cup bounced and toppled over. Ferris cursed and mopped at a brown dribble with a paper napkin. "My record is clean, Lem," he said, still looking down, "and I want to get out of here with it still clean, and maybe even with some recognition of having done a decent job. With that and without a stroke."

Ferris sighed and lobbed the wet napkin at the wastebasket. It went in. His fingers shook a little, and his vehemence surprised him.

"What is thee going to do?" Penn asked.

"There's nothin' I can do," Ferris said. "Wait. Get the damn mail out. Fill out forms."

Abruptly he hunched forward and pointed a finger at his visitor. "But, Lem, somebody's gotta look into this thing with my interests in mind. I can't do it. If I go snooping around, Harper or some other damn Inspector will be watching, and it'll look suspicious."

"What about the postmaster's league?"

Another shake. "They won't do anything unless I get hit with some official disciplinary action."

He tapped the extended finger on the desktop. "But you could do it. Will you help me, Lem?"

Penn was surprised. "What can I do, Wally? I'm a farmer. I study apples and the Bible. Thee knows I have no experience with post office, um, matters."

65

Ferris tapped his finger again. "Maybe not, but I know you, Lem Penn, and you're smarter than you look. No offense. I mean, I've heard about you going back and forth to the Middle East and wherever, talking to Arabs and Jews and whatall. Those people don't fool around over there. And I also know this isn't the first time you've been to the Hill. So you know how to look into things, find out what's true and what's eyewash."

Penn shrugged and raised his hands from the fedora on his lap, palms open. "Well, maybe so," he said, "but all that's different from murder cases and grand larceny."

A thin smile crept over his face. "But now that you mention it," he said, "I was planning to stay around town this week anyway, to prepare my talk for the Washington Meeting, and pester Abernathy about that prison some more. That always means lots of waiting for appointments. I suppose I could at least ask some questions in the meantime, see what turns up."

Penn grasped his fedora again. "I can hardly make thee any promises, though, Wally."

Ferris snorted. "I don't want promises," he growled. "You're not a damn politician. Just some information, anything to help show that nobody in this office was involved in that mess." He reached toward his back pocket. "Err, I could help you with expenses for the week," he said uncertainly.

Penn raised a hand in demurral. "No need, Wally, I'm fine. There's a room at the Quaker Committee on Congressional Concerns where I can stay, and if anything unusual comes up, I'll let thee know."

He rubbed his chin thoughtfully. "But thee wants to show that nobody here was involved, if nobody really was. Does that include the young man, Adams?"

Ferris pursed his lips. "Yeah, I guess it has to," he replied. "Like I said, I doubt he was in on it, or he never would've come back. And he's higher on Harper's suspect list than me. But if he goes down, I'll be marked too."

Penn was nodding. He stood up. "In that case," he said, "I should go talk to him first, if he's still here."

Ferris gestured with the cigarette toward the inside door. "Be my guest," he said.

66

When this guy Penn came out on the dock, I was just finishing explaining to Merle about how no job could mean no alimony and land me in jail. Merle was shaking his head, and saying, for the second or third time, "A hell of a day, ain't it? Christ, this morning we was gonna get wrote up for the pool, and that was a big deal. Who remembers it now? Jeesus."

Merle spied the newcomer, who smiled and extended a hand. "Lem Penn," he said, shaking first with Merle and then with me.

"Henderson," Merle replied. "Merle."

Penn looked at him closely. "Henderson," he said reflectively. "Thee wouldn't be from around Staunton, by any chance?"

"Sure would," Merle said. "What makes you say that?"

"Baseball," Penn answered. "Staunton was state champions in '51. And a Henderson was the star hitter. Can't recollect his first name. Was it Merle?"

"Be damned," Merle exclaimed. "That was my big brother Nate." He pushed back his American Legion cap and grinned broadly. "Goddam, Mr. Penn, you know about that?"

"I should," Penn said, "I was filling in as an umpire in the regional tournament. Staunton whipped Harrisonburg seventeen to three, and thy brother hit a grand slam home run. I was certain he'd be waving to us from a Topps baseball card next."

Merle's grin grew wistful. "He woulda, too. The scouts were watching'. But the draft got him--army draft, I mean--then a chink mortar blew off half his leg."

His face hardened. "Once he was home, 'closest Nate got to baseball was pitchin' beer bottles into the ditch."

Merle stiffened as if reflexively standing to attention. "Went in the next year myself. But 'time I got to Korea, it was mostly all over. Chinks took a few shots at me, but they missed."

Penn had been nodding sympathetically. Now he shook his head. "Too bad about thy brother," he said quietly. "There

67

was so much talent there. I remember, riding one of the buses to Richmond for the state finals. He was great there too.''

Merle was grinning again. ''Was that the bus, broke down outside o' Charlottesville? Church bus--no booze or smokin'?''

Penn chuckled. ''The one right behind, that went for help. Was thee on it?''

''Front seat. Hated it, 'cause I needed a smoke somethin' awful. But my girlfriend was a hard-core Baptist. I thought we'd never get back. Goddam, Mr. Penn, you're practically home folks. What brings you up here?''

''Wally--er, Mister Ferris asked me to look into this business of the registered mail for him.''

Merle was suddenly cautious. ''You a cop?''

A shake of the head. ''Just a friend, with some free time. Ferris thinks he's in trouble too if this missing money isn't found. So if we can clear thee, Adams, it will clear him too.''

''You got that right,'' Merle allowed. He turned to me. ''Goddam inspectors'll fry his ass if they can, son. They don't care whose nuts they nail to the wall. Ferris may be gettin' smart in his old age.''

Buoyed by Merle's agreement, Penn turned to me. ''Friend Adams--''

''Perry,'' I said, wondering why he already considered me a friend.

''Er, Perry, does thee know anything about the man who was shot, Mister, um, O'Connor?''

I shrugged, deciding to ignore his odd form of address. ''Not much. He had money, I could see that from the house. And he was always getting mail from stockbrokers, annual reports and stuff. The kind of mail I never get.''

''What was his business?''

Merle spoke up. ''Ran a security guard outfit, on contract for the gov'ment. A Beltway Bandit. The office is on Glenn's Ferry, over by the Lakeside Mall. Useta carry mail to it myself til they split it off into Route 89.''

''Herman's route,'' I said. Herman was still out on the street.

"If thee can give me the exact address, I'd like to go pay a call there," Penn said.

Merle blinked and adjusted his cap again. "Hell," he said, "for home folks I can do better'nat. I'm finished here, so I'll take you there myself. Perry, you wanna come along?"

"Why not?" I said. "I'm finished too, I guess. For the day, maybe for good. I'll drive."

"I'll tell Wally--, er Ferris, that I'm leaving," Penn said.

six

O'Connor Security Services was in one of those new townhouse office blocks, the kind with light brick veneers, narrow fronts and big bay windows.

These blocks, along with fancier developments, were going up around South Fairfax as fast as the big bulldozers could knock down the big old trees. It seemed as if every doctor, dentist, therapist, small-time professional association, consultant and mortgage hustler in the hemisphere was converging on this corner of Virginia. They were scrambling to get behind one of these front doors with a uniform-sized brass plate beside it, and then dip their buckets into the streams of Reagan war money that were sluicing through the county's streets.

It was one of the glories of the free enterprise system.

Halfway up the front steps at 3421 Glenn's Ferry, we could see through the window that nobody was there.

But more than just empty, the office looked somehow barren: a few desks, each topped with a darkened computer monitor, a keyboard, a few papers. Thick carpet covered the floor, and a row of filing cabinets stood against the back wall. A large fabric wall hanging covered much of the back wall, next to a door into an inner office. Everything was in shades of beige, including the hanging, and the whole ensemble looked as if it was trying to fade into invisibility. The only contrast came from a light flashing on a phone on the desk nearest the window.

"This place looks strange," I said. "You'd think, if his company was big enough to support that house and the life that went with it, there'd be more to it. The security guards have to report somewhere, have lockers to store their gear in. It can't be here."

"I don't know," Merle reflected. "Could be this is just his executive office. Prob'ly does the operational stuff somewheres else."

"Whatever," I said. "Anyway, looks like we wasted a trip." We headed back down the steps, toward my car.

But I felt unsatisfied, and uneasy. "What now?" I asked, pulling away.

"Dunno, Merle said. "Maybe we should put our heads together for a few minutes." He gestured toward a Roy Rogers on the next corner. "Let's get some coffee and think this over."

I was in line waiting for an order of fries when Merle, who had been ahead of me, tapped on my shoulder. "Damn, Perry, we're in luck," he muttered. "See over there?" He motioned with his steaming cup.

By the window a woman sat in a low booth, her face turned away from us to stare out the window. She had a long brown ponytail and a beige pantsuit, and one finger was slowly tracing circles on the rim of her coffee cup, which looked cold.

"That's his secretary," Merle whispered.

"You know her?"

"To say hello," he shrugged. "Can't hurt."

It didn't. He and Penn were seated across from her when I came over. She glanced up at me. "Did you really see--it happen?" she asked without preamble.

I nodded. She was next to pretty, with a longish face and large brown eyes behind horn-rimmed glasses. There was a hint of country in her speech that I couldn't quite place, but which undercut the sophisticated look of her outfit and hair. "It was pretty scary," I said, feeling the remark's inanity, but not knowing anything better to say.

"Barbara Keene," Penn said quietly, "Perry Adams." He seemed to be in charge of the conversation already. Then to her, resuming a line of questioning I had interrupted:

"Thee said thee'd been working there--?"

"Pretty near four years," she answered, turning back to face him. "It was a good place to work, mostly."

70

There was an earnestness in her voice and an openness in her expression that surprised me, considering that she was facing three strangers, all but Merle completely unfamiliar.

"Mostly?" Penn queried, looking quizzical.

Watching her, though, I realized she was largely ignoring Merle and me, focussed instead on Penn. She leaned toward him as she spoke, and her hands seemed to be reaching for his across the table, as if for comfort, or to keep from falling.

"Sure," she said, "the pay wasn't bad to start, and I got raises ever' six months. That was darn good for just a secretary, in a recession as tough as it's been til recently. Good health insurance too. I had a hernia operation last year. It paid ever' darn penny."

She let out a long sigh. "So I can't complain about all that. 'Course," she grinned shamefacedly, "he was always coming on to me, you know."

"He--?" said Penn.

"Gil," she said, and her hands jerked up a few inches in a What-can-you-do? gesture. "Ray never bothered me."

A glance at me. "Ray's the manager." Then back to Penn. "But Gil was a real pain sometimes. Especially after he split up with his wife."

She picked up her coffee, sipped it, and grimaced at the cold. "She called him a lot, usually mad as all get out, and she was real hostile to me. 'Guess she just figured I was one o' his bimbos."

Her bottom lip trembled briefly. "But I wasn't," she quavered. "Never. So at least he could take no for an answer."

A shaky sigh. "Even if I did have to keep repeating it. And--" Another pause. "Gil was real good about letting me go to school. I been taking courses at George Mason right along. He always encouraged me, and last year the company paid half my tuition. I wanna try for law school, after I graduate next year."

She looked over at me again, defiantly. "Not bad for a girl from Summit Point, West Virginia. It beats working at the race track..."

"Or the apple warehouse," Penn murmured. "I know

Summit Point.''

She looked at him with anguish in her face. Her lower lip was trembling again, and now her eyes were filling. "First one in my family to get a degree," she wailed. "Or I was gonna be. Now I don't know what--"

Penn handed her a napkin. She pushed up her glasses and leaned her eyes into it.

"I had a good thing going there," she sobbed from behind the napkin. "Now what do I do?"

"I'm sure thee'll find something else," Penn soothed.

She wiped her eyes and blew her nose. "You think so?" she asked, in a little girl tone.

"No doubt about it," he answered cheerfully. "I know Summit Point. They make 'em tough there. Thee'll be fine."

She smiled weakly at him, somehow reassured. He moved on.

"Can thee tell us anything about the operation, Barbara? Where did the security guards actually report? Who hired them?"

"Oh, Ray handled all that," she said vaguely. "They had an office in Springfield too. We--Gil, I mean--mostly worked on the contracts here. Gil was mainly a salesman, you know, always lining up more work. Ray ran the operation."

She frowned thoughtfully. "Actually," she said, "even Ray didn't handle all that much actual security work. He subcontracted most of it out to other outfits."

Merle spoke up. "So Mr. O'Connor was more kind of a broker, eh?"

She nodded. "I guess that's right. Everybody seemed happy with the arrangement, though. Gil kept bringing in more contracts, and everybody had more work." She sipped her coffee again. "There was plenty of work, all right. The past couple years I could hardly keep up with it."

"This fellow Ray," Penn asked, "where would we find him?"

A shrug. "Don't know. Haven't seen him all day. He's not really in his office that much."

"Ray who?" Merle inquired.

"Musto," she said. "He called in once for messages,

72

said he was at the Advanced Naval Research Center--it's over in Arlington. Said there was some kind of contract hassle he was working out.'' Her eyebrows came together. ''Come to think of it, he sounded real edgy. It wasn't like him.''

''What about O'Connor's ex-wife?'' I put in. ''Did she call today?''

She looked toward me. ''Yes, come to think of it, she did. First thing this morning. Sounded mad as hell about something, as always. She sells real estate, and calls him at least once a week, usually on her car phone.''

''Did she say anything about...?'' Penn ventured, but the pony tail shook vigorously.

''Like I said, she assumes I'm his girlfriend, so she doesn't have much to say to me.''

She glanced down at her wristwatch. ''Oh, god!'' she yelped. ''My paralegal's class starts in fifteen minutes. I gotta get outta here.'' She reached for her coffee cup, but Penn waved her away with a gesture that said he'd take care of it.

''We appreciate thy time, friend Barbara,'' he said.

She looked at him again, plaintively this time. ''Is my mascara all smeared?'' she asked. Her voice was small, little girlish. I realized that he somehow came across to her with a kind of beloved old uncle's charisma.

''It's okay,'' he said. ''But check it when thee gets the chance.''

Good legs, I thought, as she pushed through the glass door. When I noticed Merle watching too, I said, ''Well?''

''Nice,'' he commented.

''But what about--?''

He spread his hands in a sign of ignorance.

Penn shoved her coffee cup through the slot of a square white trash bin. He came back to the table, looking pensive.

''I can think of at least two possible reasons why this Ray Musto might have been edgy on the phone today,'' he said quietly.

''Such as?'' I asked.

''Well,'' he said, ''for one, a congressional committee that Richard Abernathy is on has some kind of interest in this

73

company. They got a call about the murder while I was in his office, possibly from whoever found the body. When I thought about that, I remembered reading that Abernathy chairs the Government Operations investigative subcommittee that's been looking into defense contract irregularities.'' He raised his eyebrows. ''Suppose those two facts are connected?

''Suppose they are,'' I said. ''That could be heavy.''

''What's the second reason?'' Merle pressed.

Penn looked surprised. He spread his hands, as if it was obvious. ''What if he had just killed O'Connor. Or was just about to.''

seven

Back at the station, we walked Penn to his car, an ageless gray Valiant. ''We need to know more about O'Connor, and what interested Abernathy about him,'' Penn said. ''I'll make some calls in Washington tomorrow. And there should be some records at the Reference Service at the Library of Congress that will help.''

Merle rubbed his chin as the old car chugged out of the South Fairfax lot. I could tell he was thinking hard.

''Yeah?'' I prodded.

''Two things,'' he said.

''Number One?''

''Number one,'' Merle said, ''what does that guy do to women? That Barbara opened up to him like he was her long lost dad. Never seen anything like it.''

''I noticed that too,'' I said. ''It was almost eerie. Wonder if I could borrow some of it.''

Merle snorted. ''Come back in twenty years,'' he said.

''I suppose,'' I sighed. ''What about Number Two?''

''Number Two,'' Merle said, ''you need to find out some more about this O'Connor guy too. And not from no damn library.

''And what does that mean?''

Merle squeezed his lips together and pushed them out into an inverted V; more concentration.

74

"It means, for one thing, that 4936, one lousy little yellow slip of paper, could get you out of this mess real quick. Ferris too."

"Sure." I didn't see his point. "If we could find it. But it's gone, remember?"

Merle shot me a look between narrowed lids. "But gone where? Suppose we found it?"

"How are we supposed--" I stopped, and my eyes narrowed. "Just exactly who is 'we'? And what do you have in mind?"

"I'm thinkin'," he said, "that you're gonna need some help. And I owe you one. So I suggest you meet me in the parking lot at Ferris's Country Store at ten o'clock tonight."

"You serious?"

"Did Staunton win that damn ballgame?" he snapped. "Show up, and try me."

eight

When I got home, it was almost seven.

Home is a studio mini-flat, in a basement corner under a crackerbox house in South Arlington, with the entrance in the back. I think it's illegal, because the rent is very reasonable for the area, and the driveway goes all the way round to the back of the house, so I park away from the prying eyes of any building inspectors.

Inside, long bookshelves of bricks and boards line two of the four walls of my single large room, the pine lumber sagging under the load. The sofabed and my desk, an old kitchen door bridging a pair of two-drawer filing cabinets, are against the third wall, and what passes as a kitchen covers the rest. The bathroom is outside, hard by the washer and dryer.

The only high-tech items in my digs were a secondhand Kaypro computer, a new microwave oven, and a square black Sony answering machine.

I turned to the Sony first, because the blinking light on its tiny console gave me hope.

Nor was I disappointed. The one message on the tape

was a familiar voice, with undertones of teasing as well as seduction.

"Sorry I wasn't here today," Jennifer said. "But tomorrow the boys are going on a field trip to the Aquarium in Baltimore, and they won't get back til late. I'll be working til noon, so I can't go along to help the teachers. Can you come by, say, early afternoon? Bye."

I smiled and opened the refrigerator. A clear plastic pitcher half-filled with orange juice had separated and turned slightly brown. The top two American cheese slices in the open pack were curling stiffly upward. I wished I had brought home a pizza; but the need to stretch my meager bank balance was already weighing me down.

There was half a loaf of bread, though, and the bottom slices of the cheese were still passable.

A microwave melted cheese sandwich would have to do it.

Then a nap, before whatever Merle had in mind.

And tomorrow afternoon: A roll in the hay.

CHAPTER FIVE

one

Viewed from Route 77, South Fairfax is a paradoxical place. From the larger roads, it looks like what it now is: a freshly-minted suburb for the newly affluent, home to the winners of the Reagan Era.

But turn an obscure corner here and there, following the mail, and the road turns abruptly to rutty gravel, and the mailboxes rusty and battered. Then, for a few hundred yards, behind the screen of woods, you're suddenly somewhere else:

In an outpost of Appalachia, for instance, confronted by a peak-roofed clapboard house sagging a little to leeward and just this side of being a shack. A Confederate flag painted on an aluminum sheet is nailed over the screen door. A wheelless car sits on blocks in the yard. A silvery beer keg is stuck in the crotch of a tree ten feet above the ground.

I've yet to see what the inhabitants of this particular estate look like; but I can tell you their mail doesn't include *Town and Country* or *The Wall Street Journal.*

The rutted lane loops past this apparition, twists back on itself through the trees, and rejoins Fox Run Shoals. From there it's barely a stone's throw to the wide and elegantly-hedged asphalt of Quarterhorse Gateway, which winds smoothly around a row of sprawling mansions. The residents here include the French-speaking deputy Ambassador from somewhere with oil, and a certified Amway soap tycoon--a Triple Diamond, I think.

The woods mask such jarring juxtapositions, and enable the ambassador and the soap mogul to stay oblivious to the area's aboriginal inhabitants. I doubt that the folks at the house with the rebel flag are unaware of their new neighbors; such indifference is an amenity of wealth, as invisibility is a feature of poverty.

Another anomalous enclave hidden among the trees is

Commonwealth Road. It's even easier to miss, because no houses are visible, just a row of shabby mailboxes perched like arthritic crows on a weathered wooden fence next to what looks like a gate into a fallow field.

But follow the gravel track through the field and down a short slope, as I did once with a cert from Social Security for a Mrs. Habersham, and you pass a dozen or so small houses, half of them empty, all run-down, and several inarguably shacks. And every one is, or was, occupied by a black family.

Blacks are so rare in this Zip Code that the only possible explanation for their presence is that they were here first, maybe as far back as Reconstruction--and for that matter, most of the residents look as if they could remember those days. That included Mrs. Habersham, who came slowly toward the door, carefully gripping an aluminum walker, and signed the 4936 in a crabbed scrawl that could well have been a shaky X. Looking at me through thick filmy lenses, she allowed that she'd have to wait til her granddaughter got home from school to read the missive.

There's a story in this place, I thought then.

two

I thought it again when Merle slowed at the row of mailboxes and pulled into the field on Monday night.

He had abandoned his jeep in favor of a quieter old chevy, and we slid almost noiselessly past the first several houses.

"Average age here is seventy-five or so," he said. "Mos' these folks are too confused to notice the car, and the rest are deaf. They won't bother us." He pulled into the rutted drive at the last house and stopped. It was dark and cold.

"Folks here been dead for years," he said.

"Why hasn't the place been sold and developed?" I wondered.

"Can't," he said. "Not yet. All the houses here are owned by a trust, so they have to wait 'em out, til the old ones die and they c'n buy the whole batch from the kids."

"Lucky for the kids," I said. "That oughta be a bundle for college."

"Yep. And right now it's handy for us." He pointed to the windshield and opened the door. "The path is right behind the house. Useta hunt squirrels out here before all the new houses went up."

I saw his breath steam when he stepped out on the gravel. "You sure about this?" I said, for about the fourth time. "Breaking and entering was still illegal, last I heard."

"Don't be such a damn pussy," he taunted. "Piece o' cake."

I peered past him into the darkness. Through the trees were new houses, those on Bluebird Lane. In particular, Gilbert O'Connor's at 2306. It was the closest to us, at the end of the lane, just a hundred yards or so through the woods, though light years away on the cultural and class maps.

I couldn't see it through the trees; no lights on. But an arc lamp further up the slope flickered through the huddled bare branches. Probably by Kasabian's gate, I guessed. I hoped the Nazi dogs were upwind from us. And asleep.

"Come on," Merle murmured. He set off around the house, crouching slightly. I hesitated a second, then zipped up my jacket and followed.

The path through the trees was well-worn and easy to follow, even in the dark. I wondered if any of the working age residents of Commonwealth Road had trod it to work as domestics in the big houses on Bluebird Lane. It would figure.

It seemed only a minute before Merle paused and whispered over his shoulder, "Fence. Just boards. Step careful." He lifted one leg, hoisted himself lightly over and thumped on the other side. I scrambled after him.

Now there was the muffled crunch of frosted grass underfoot, and the arc light vanished behind a looming black oblong ahead of us.

"Big back yard," I said. Then we were on a patio, the concrete ghostly in the night. I stopped. "Won't there be an alarm?" I said.

"Probably turned off," Merle whispered. "Lemme check." He crossed the patio to a set of sliding glass doors, and leaned in close, examining something I couldn't see. Then he pulled on the handle, and half turned toward me. His teeth gleamed in a grin. "No problem, buddy." Pushing to his left, the glass panel slid away from him. He stepped inside.

Again, I followed. It was pitch black, and I bumped into him. "Steady," he hissed.

"How did you open it?" I asked.

"Simple," he whispered. "Wasn't locked. I think the killer came in this way. Cops probably didn't find the key, and they figgered that whatever was really valuable in the place was already gone."

"They were probably right," I said, feeling more and more spooked. "How did you guess they'd leave it unlocked?"

"I was a MP in Korea. I seen cops do all kinda stupid things. So it 'as worth a try." I heard him fumbling in his jacket pocket. "Here," he handed me a small piece of cold square plastic.

He clicked on the bright narrow beam of a pocket flash. I clicked mine.

We were in the master bedroom. The place was a shambles. In our slender shafts of light a king-size bed dominated the space, with papers and clothes strewn on and around it.

"I figgered the place'd be tossed," Merle said. "Prob'ly cut off the alarm too. Wasn't even set."

"Who would've done it?"

"The cops. The killer. Maybe both. Or maybe somebody else with a key's been here since then."

I raised my light and swung it around the room. Something flashed on the wall, and I moved the light back to it: The glass frame of a large diploma or certificate. I stepped toward it and read from the ornately calligraphed script.

"Outstanding Alumnus Award, 1984. St. Joseph's Military Academy, Easton Maryland. *'Principium sapientiae. Pr 4:7.'*" O'Connor's name was underneath.

"Merle," I whispered, "do you read Latin?"

He snorted. "What kinda dumb-ass question is that?" His beam flicked to the frame, then darted into other corners of the room. "Come on," he growled, "we'ain't come here for language lessons. Let's get busy."

He stepped to the other side of the bed and sat down on its edge. He aimed his flash at the hallway which led toward the kitchen and the front door. "There's bloodstains in the hall," he said. The light bounced jerkily back over the carpet. "Here, too. Guy musta staggered back this way 'fore he croaked."

He put his flash down and I heard him feeling around on the bed. "What is it?"

"Somethin' funny here," he said. He stood and bent over, feeling between the mattress and the box spring. Then he sucked in his breath. "Hot damn," he said. "Come to papa. Perry, bring your light."

I went over and shined the flash on his hands. He was holding a small cardboard box. One end had been ripped open, and it was crushed almost flat by the weight of the mattress, but when Merle turned it over in his hands the red Registered label was still there. I drew in a breath.

Merle looked in the open end, then pulled out a folded sheet of paper. He glanced at it, then handed it to me.

It was headed "Blumstein & Co., 3 Broad Street, New York, New York," and it was the financial equivalent of a packing list. It said the parcel had contained $756,000 in currency and bearer bonds. It added that an additional $345,000 had been forwarded separately to a safety deposit box at the Banco Central Costariccensa in San Jose, Costa Rica. Instructions for gaining access to the box would be waiting for him at the front desk of the San Jose Hilton. Blumstein's fee of $10,000, it advised, had already been deducted from the total of funds realized in the transactions.

I whistled. "This is more money than I ever thought I'd get my hands on," I said.

"'Cept you don't have your hands on it," Merle said.

"Not now," I agreed, "but I had it this morning. Jesus." The thought made my palms tingle.

The tingle reminded me of something else. "So where's the 4936?" I folded the sheet and turned back toward the mattress. "Damn the money. That slip's what we came for."

I felt around under the mattress. Nothing. "Help me lift this thing up," I said, motioning for Merle to raise one end.

81

We had one long side of the mattress up and pointed toward the ceiling, and were playing our flashes across its quilted underside when the Nazi dogs started baying up the road. They barked once, then again, then stopped.

Their howling was subdued and half-hearted, and I was about to ignore it when gravel crunched at the end of the long drive.

Merle flicked off his flash. I hesitated. "I don't see it," I whispered urgently. I didn't want to quit searching. I felt that the 4936 was close, almost within reach.

"Cut the light, dammit!" Merle was tense. "Time to make like a shepherd. Get the flock outta here."

Reluctantly I turned off the light and started for the glass doors. But in the dark I misjudged the dimensions of the oversized bed and stumbled over the corner. Reaching to steady myself, I felt the folded letter flutter from my grasp. "Dammit!" I muttered, and started feeling around frantically for it.

Merle tugged at my jacket. *"Come on,"* he commanded. Cold air poured in as the glass doors slid open. Then we were crossing the pale squares of the patio, and trotting on the frost-stiffened grass.

Once over the board fence, Merle turned and crouched. "Shhh," he said, pulling me down beside him.

We peered back toward the house, and after a few seconds I could see another flashlight beam moving inside it. The light flickered in the hallway, and then showed in the master bedroom. Then, abruptly, it dimmed and vanished.

Merle grunted. "Pulled the curtains over the glass doors," he murmured. "I didn't stop to think about that."

I was shivering. "Let's go," I said. "Before they come looking out here."

Merle found the path between the trees as easily as if it had been broad daylight.

Back in my car, I pounded my fist on the steering wheel as we drove past the darkened houses on Commonwealth Lane. For a second I could see Mrs. Habersham, gripping her walker, and wondered if she was still alive. But then she faded.

"It felt so close, Merle. I'm sure that yellow slip was

82

there. You don't suppose whoever came in was hunting for it too, do you?''

Merle shook his head. ''Not unless it was Ferris,'' he said. ''Which I doubt. They probably wanted the money, or some kind of incriminating evidence.''

''But they already got the money,'' I protested. ''That was the whole point. Wasn't it?''

''Sure,'' Merle said. ''But *who's* got it?'' He scratched at his forehead. ''And who else *wants* it?'' His lips were screwing up again, as they had when he dreamed up this caper. ''And evidently, somebody else wants something in that house pretty bad.''

He scratched again, this time at his stubbly chin. ''Perry, ole buddy, this business is getting down-goddam-right interesting.''

The heater hadn't kicked in yet. I blew on my cold fingers. ''Yeah. But I still wish we'd found that damned slip.''

three

Shortly after ten o'clock Tuesday morning, Richmond Bacon Hadley wiped his watery eyes with a large handkerchief and put his thick glasses back on. Squinting out the window of the third-floor office at The Quaker Committee on Congressional Concerns, he saw the dome of the Capitol, white and familiar two blocks west.

Somehow he never tired of that vista. Glancing down, he also saw Lemuel Penn coming down the sidewalk.

Hadley sighed, lifted his glasses and dabbed again with the handkerchief.

He was not weeping; he was not even sad. His eyes simply were red and watery a lot nowadays. It was one more sign of the toll eighty-five years of wear and tear had taken on even as sturdy a Midwestern farmer's frame as his.

Hadley knew that what Penn saw as he mounted the steps was a nondescript three-story townhouse with peeling paint. When QCCC bought the place in 1961, at Hadley's insistence, many of his Oversight Committee members thought he was crazy:

83

Sure, it's cheap, they said, *and it should be--the place is a dump, in the middle of a dangerous black slum. No congressman or staffer in their right minds will ever go near it.*

Hadley recalled that Penn had been on the committee then, a crucial swing vote--though of course in the Quaker style they made decisions by sense of the meeting, without formally counting heads. But when Hadley had managed to persuade Penn, the thrifty apple farmer, that the location had a future and was a risk worth taking, Penn's support was crucial in bringing the committee around.

Once the deed was done, the committee rallied to fix up the place, mainly with volunteer labor. The staff, consisting then of Hadley, a secretary, and a couple of volunteer retirees, moved into the first floor and kept on with their work. Their goal was nothing less than to persuade Congress to end the draft, wind down the Cold War, and drastically cut the military budget.

The committee didn't notice until later that the purchase had begun a turnaround of the entire neighborhood. The term "gentrification" hadn't been invented yet, and it rankled Hadley now, but that's what they had done.

The recollection brought a thin smile to Hadley's wrinkled face. Between here and the corner Penn had walked past several recently planted high-ticket lobbying offices and a clutch of gold-plated rehabs, all salted with ex-congressmen and other VIP wannabes. In such upscale company, the QCCC building once again looked rather down at the heels. But Hadley and the other staff, which now filled most of the building, were inured to Quaker frugality and plainness and mainly indifferent to its appearance, except when a slate fell off the roof or a pipe broke inside.

Nor did they much care that the property was now worth several million of the new lobbyists' dollars, enough to set QCCC up in bigger, fancier digs out in Fairfax or Silver Spring. Hadley knew, and by now the Oversight Committee did too, that any such site Beyond the Beltway, no matter how spaciously elegant, would be a net loser in access and influence. QCCC's close proximity to the Hill was a more authentic status symbol than a big suburban spread, and was, moreover, one they had earned honestly. Thus

84

the real estate fever now sweeping the Hill neighborhood, as it was most of metropolitan Washington, had passed them by.

Instead, QCCC stuck doggedly to its quiet lobbying. And if Hadley could rarely point to much in the way of concrete results for all his efforts, he had, on the other hand, not lost hope. He smiled again, ruefully, recalling how in thirty years work against the draft, he had never gotten more than ten votes to end it on the floor. But nevertheless, and hallelujah, the draft was now more than ten years gone. And of all people, it was Richard Nixon, the renegade Quaker president, who had stopped it.

The Lord works in mysterious ways, Hadley had told the committee then. *We must never lose hope.*

The Pentagon budget was another matter. Scaling it back was a will-o-the-wisp in the best of times. But this mission seemed particularly impossible once Ronald Reagan swept into town. Would the man, Hadley wondered, never stop throwing billions down that dangerous rathole like there was no tomorrow?

Hadley had voted Democrat for president fourteen times, ever since Herbert Hoover, the first Quaker president, had disappointed him. But his ancestral Iowa Republican streak was deeply offended by the sheer waste of all that tax money, and the ballooning national debt that was its legacy.

Of course, being ten years older than the incumbent president, Hadley was officially retired now. He hadn't wanted to let go; but in 1979 the Oversight Committee finally said the time had come.

Very well, he had told them, *you're probably right. But I've been working fulltime for disarmament since 1937, and with the world arming faster than ever, you can't really expect me to stop now.*

And he hadn't. For Richmond Bacon Hadley, retirement had made only three significant changes:

First, he now got a pension check instead of a salary.

Second, his old suits had grown even shinier with continued wear.

And third, he had moved from the less than luxurious first floor Executive Secretary's office to the downright spartan volunteer quarters on the third floor.

Here, at a secondhand oak desk, pecking at a donated IBM PC and sharing a telephone with the other volunteers, he soldiered on. For fifty to sixty hours a week, he wrote letters, made calls and attended meetings, still trying to roll back the tide of militarism.

He lifted his glasses and wiped his eyes again.

Richmond Bacon Hadley was not sad. But he was, he now occasionally admitted to himself, beginning to get tired.

He recognized Penn's slow step coming up the stairs, and then the telephone ended his reverie.

Hadley reached for it eagerly. Just maybe, it would be the Deputy Assistant Secretary of Defense for Policy Planning, ready at last to hear about the alternative estimates of Soviet military strength Hadley had turned up. Or perhaps the young fellow over at State who was part of the SALT missile talks....

"This is Marge Capriotti?" said a strange nasal voice that rose interrogatively at the end of each phrase. "At the Advanced Naval Research Center? I'm looking for a Mr. Penn? Is he there?"

Hadley sighed, and glanced out the window again.

"Hold on," he said. "Penn is just coming in."

He swiveled toward the door. "Lem? It's for you."

four

Penn was at the offices of O'Connor Security Services by ten. They looked even more beige and barren from the inside, he reflected. Except by the front desk, where Barbara Keene smiled warmly up at him. Her dark hair and eyes, not so remarkable in themselves, gave contrast and definition to her portion of the room. Even the remains of her breakfast, a croissant's crumpled foil wrapper by a red and orange Roy Rogers bag, seemed to brighten the place, give it life. She had been reading Tuesday's *Wall Street Journal*.

Barbara Keene hung up the beige phone. "Ray will be right out," she said. "How's your investigation going?"

Penn smiled back and shrugged. "Nothing much to report yet," he said. The remark sounded inane, he thought, but it was also true. "How was your class last night?" More inanity.

But she seemed pleased that he remembered. "Great," she said. "I aced a quiz."

"Good," Penn said. He hesitated briefly, then decided to venture beyond the inanity. "How does it look here," he said, a little diffidently. "For you, I mean."

Her brows began to knit. But before she could answer, the door in the back by the big beige wall hanging opened, and a tall slender man with greying hair and an olive complexion came toward them.

Ray Musto was in shirtsleeves, with a bow tie and suspenders, a sheaf of papers in one hand and a preoccupied expression. His face was long, with round glasses above a thick black mustache. He stubbed out a cigarette in a well-filled ashtray. "Mr. Penn," he said, extending the other hand, "Barbara told me about you." He gestured toward the door. "Come in."

Compared to the cautiously neutral decor outside, Musto's office was a riot of color: large travel posters dominated three walls, each a mediterranean scene: Athens, Crete, Istanbul. His desk was covered with papers. The formality of his dress looked somewhat out of place there, but he slipped easily into the chair behind the desk. And he spoke directly to the point, skipping decorous small talk. "Have they caught the killer yet?"

Penn shook his head.

"Terrible thing," Musto said. "He was my friend, you know, as well as my boss. He built this company singlehanded, and I don't know how long we'll be able to go on without him."

Penn nodded sympathetically. "When did thee last see him?" he asked.

"See him?" Musto echoed. "Lemme think. Saturday. He came in for awhile, we were working on a proposal."

"What about talking to him?"

"Yesterday morning. I called from the Advanced Naval Research Center in Arlington. We have a large contract there, with some problems."

"About what time was that?"

Musto frowned in thought. "Hm, before ten. I guess I

87

might have been the last one to talk to him, before--'' he stopped. ''I hadn't thought of that before. Jesus, how do these things happen?''

''Did Mr. O'Connor have any enemies?''

Musto shrugged. ''He and his ex-wife didn't get along. But I don't think--''

The phone on his desk buzzed. He picked it up. ''Yes, Barbara?'' He listened, and then glanced up at Penn. ''It's Arlington,'' he whispered. ''More problems.'' Then, into the phone, ''Okay, put him on.''

Musto leaned back and seemed to focus on the fleecy clouds above a spotless curving beach on the poster of Crete. ''Yeah, Ted,'' he boomed cheerily. ''How's it going?''

The response was lengthy, and Musto's expression seemed to tighten around his professional smile. After several minutes, marked by only noncommital murmurs of response, he cupped a hand over the mouthpiece and shifted his gaze to his visitor. ''Mr. Penn, this is going to take awhile,'' he said apologetically. Could we--''

Penn rose. ''I'll get back to thee,'' he said easily, shook Musto's hand quickly, and turned to go.

''Look, Ted,'' Musto said from behind him, weariness creeping into his voice, ''I'm sure we can--''

The door closed.

Barbara was also on the phone, and Penn waved to her as he left. He too was preoccupied now.

Starting up his Valiant, he asked himself why Musto would have lied so boldly. For Penn knew, courtesy of Marge Capriotti, that Ray Musto had not arrived at the Advanced Naval Research Center until midafternoon. Had he stretched the time to establish an alibi?

Penn wanted to report to Walter Ferris. But as he passed the Roy Rogers, a sign on the lawn of a house across the road reminded him that he needed to make one more stop first.

five

88

"Where was thee when it--happened?" Penn asked cautiously.

"Working," Ruth Solomon, nee O'Connor, answered. "I had a guy almost ready to sign a contract on a new colonial, over by the shopping center. He stalled at the last minute, said he wanted to talk to his wife again, but I think he was almost ready."

She turned to face him. Her expression showed a mix of confusion and surprise at herself. "Why," she asked, "am I telling you all this?"

They were at the wrought iron gate of 2306 Bluebird Lane. With the confidence of an experienced real estate agent, Ruth was turning her key in the lock, ignoring the yellow police ribbon across it. The gate opened with a quiet scrape, and she pushed the ribbon aside.

Penn had no immediate answer. It was remarkable, the way she had begun opening up to him, a complete stranger, as if he were a favorite uncle or father confessor, almost from the moment she picked him up at Ferris's Store. When he mentioned that he'd like to see the house, she had driven her silver-grey Accord straight there.

They were, he noted, a distinctly mismatched pair: he in his worn suit, she smart in the successful businesswoman's uniform of navy jacket and skirt, softened by a white blouse with a large bow. Her black hair was cut short and her mascara was thick, and Penn thought he could catch a fading glimpse of Liza Minelli in her eyes when she looked sidelong at him.

"Perhaps," he said as they moved past the shattered glass front door, "I remind thee of someone--"

She studied him for a moment, narrowing her eyes. She was carefully made up, with earrings that dangled and sparkled when her head moved.

"Zeyde," she said softly.

"What?"

"Zeyde," she repeated. "Yiddish for grandfather. You look a little like him. He was always good to me. I ran to him when my brother picked on me. Maybe that's it."

Penn nodded acceptance of this speculation. He didn't

89

feel like her grandfather, but his task was to gain the most from her openness, not analyze it away.

"What a mess," she said, stepping around the pieces of glass on the bloodstained carpet. "I'll get it cleaned up as soon as the cops will let me back in officially. They said it wouldn't be long, but what does that mean?"

She led him into the large master bedroom, which was still in disarray. Penn's attention, though, was drawn to the large framed certificate on the wall by the bed.

"*Principium sapientiae,*" he murmured. "'Wisdom is the principal thing.' The Book of Proverbs."

"That was his high school," Ruth said. "Catholic military academy out on the Eastern Shore. Went there on a scholarship. He always said it was what got him out of the slums of Baltimore, gave him his start. Gil was not interested in charities, but he gave them a lot of money. Headed the campaign to double their scholarship fund, and put up half the money himself."

She moved to the end of the bed, and from a tangled pile of clothing pulled out a oversized sweatshirt. On it was printed the same logo as the certificate, and under it the words, "Class of '83."

"He insisted on sending our son there. We fought about it. I didn't want Ted to go. Why should he leave his mother at that tender age? And I don't like Catholic schools. So we compromised, and he went his last two years of high school."

"And where is Ted now?"

"Virginia Tech. Says he's going to be an engineer." She let the sweatshirt drop and sat down on the edge of the bed. "It was just as well he went over to Easton," she said, and her voice started to crack. "Things were so bad here, he was better off not hearing us screaming and fighting. I moved out in October of '82, his senior year." She sighed. "They practically had to have military escorts to keep us apart at his graduation."

Penn reached into a box of tissues on a bedside table and handed her one. She dabbed at her eyes, trying to preserve her mascara.

"If thee doesn't mind my asking," Penn ventured, "what

90

made things so bad then?"

Ruth gave him a sharp look, then swept an arm in an arc. "This!" she said. "Look at the place. Phony pretentious California gaudiness. I never liked it."

"The house?" Penn was not at confused as he sounded. He was trying to draw her out.

She shrugged, one arm still outstretched. "Well, not just the house. The whole thing. So much money, so fast. When Gil started the company, it was a mom-and-pop thing. He was at Towson State, working as a security guard to get through. He'd been an MP in the army. I met him there, at Towson."

She drew her head back, her earrings swinging, looking at him defiantly. "If you want to know the truth, I flunked out of Goucher. My good Jewish parents were mortified: their only daughter was not going to be a doctor or a lawyer after all. A teacher if they were lucky."

"And then thee married a Catholic."

Her chuckle was bitter. "Worse than that, Mr. Penn. A Catholic Republican. To my parents, Franklin Roosevelt was the greatest man since Moses. But I think Gil and Pat Buchanan were hatched from the same litter. My folks hardly spoke to me for the first three years we were married. Til Ted was born."

She stood up, and made her way to a low dresser against the far wall. She picked up a picture frame that was face down on it, and moved around the bed to hand it to Penn.

The youth in the photo was mildly handsome, dark haired, with an almost winning smile. "A fine boy," Penn murmured. "I can understand why he brought thy parents around."

She smiled at this, but as she did so, a tear slipped from her lashes. She sat down on the bed again, and put her hands to her eyes. "Oh, damn my makeup," she said, and sobbed quietly.

Penn took a step and put a hand on her shoulder. He felt a bit awkward, alone in this strange house with a weeping woman. Just remember Zeyde, he reminded himself. "Thee doesn't have to talk about it anymore," he said soothingly. "We can go if thee likes."

She pulled away from his hand. "No!" It was almost a

shout. "I want to talk about it, don't you see? I want to!" Her eyes, reddened now, were rimmed with dark streaks.

"I want to, because no matter what my parents thought, it was good at first. We were together. The business was small, just a couple of contracts. But it was growing. Gil was a hustler, always schmoozing and sniffing for business. I didn't mind, then. I worked from home, did all the bookkeeping, answered the phone, sometimes changing Ted's diapers at the same time. It was tough, but we were together. A family." She sniffed. "Give me another kleenex."

Penn handed her the box, and she grabbed several. "When did it--change?" he asked.

"After the '80 election," she said. "He hated Carter, and early in the campaign he found out that one of his old St. Joseph's classmates was tied in with Bill Casey. Casey's a big Catholic, you know. So Gil got himself introduced, and gave them some money. Not much as those things go, but a lot for us, and we were in the right place at the right time. After Reagan got in, it paid off. Gil had contacts, he had done his bit and they were glad he wasn't looking for a job, just ins with contractors."

She shrugged again. "After that, the floodgates just opened. I never saw so much money move so fast. And the more there was, the more he wanted."

"Didn't thee want it too?"

"At first," she said. "But it got out of hand. All of a sudden he had an office, with his own secretary, that young bimbo--"

"Barbara," Penn said.

"--Oh, so you've had the pleasure," she hissed.

Penn smiled sheepishly. "She seemed nice enough," he said.

"Nice," Ruth repeated. "I'll bet she was nice. And nice in his bed too."

"For the record," Penn felt obliged to say, "she said they were never involved, though Gil often asked."

"Yeah, well that's at least half true," Ruth said. "I'm sure he asked. But if she said no, which I still doubt, there were others who said yes." Another sob. "Lots of them."

"Was that why you left?"

She nodded and wiped her eyes again. "But not all of it. Once I was out of the office, and the money came rolling in, the whole thing started to bother me."

"What 'whole thing'?"

"The business. It began to smell wrong."

"Wrong?" he prompted. There was something she didn't want to say.

She glared at him. "All right, crooked. I think he was paying people off to get business. Over the table, under the table, both. You might have noticed that his office is almost empty. He really became just a middleman, mostly packaging contracts for smaller companies, taking his cut as they passed by. Why would the bigger guys do that, unless they were getting a payback too?"

She stood, returned to the dresser, and fetched another framed photo. Penn recognized the Vice President between two other men, all in evening dress. Ruth leered at it.

"That's Gil on the left. So all of a sudden he's a big Republican moneybags. Invited to the bigwigs' parties, the kind you pay thousands to go to. We even went to the White House for dinner in early '82. I hated it. And Gil hated that I hated it."

She tossed the photo back toward the dresser. It overshot, bounced off the wall, and clattered to the floor.

Ruth smirked at it, then looked sidelong at Penn. "I don't really care that much about politics. But I know I'm not one of them. I don't know which ones made me the maddest--the self-righteous nouveau riche types going on about welfare and how they'd been born again, or the WASPy country clubbers, snickering at the nouveaus and everybody else. The way they all talked about Democrats gave me the creeps, because they were talking about my folks. I kept thinking I'd never be able to face my parents again, associating with that crowd."

She sighed again. "But Gil loved it. And he made it pay. Then the smell of money drew younger women, like flies to dog poop."

"So thee--left," Penn said.

She held her hands out to him, cupped as if handing him a bowl. "Yeah. After I caught him here with some bimbo. But

93

you see, it all went together somehow. I can't really explain it."

"I think thee's done very well at explaining it," Penn said. He looked around the room. "And now, what's thee going to do with all of it?"

She followed his gaze, then looked straight at him. "I may not get to do anything with it, Mr. Penn," her voice was tired. "It may not belong to me. None of it. Gil fought me every inch of the way during the divorce. The final property settlement is still pending in the district court."

She swept her arm around. "I haven't seen his will yet. He might have left everything to Ted." She nodded toward the framed certificate. "Or maybe to St. Joseph's." Her eyes narrowed again. "But it's just as likely that it's all mortgaged to the hilt, and there may be nothing left but debts."

She turned and walked toward the glass doors. Pulling the dark curtains back, she gazed across the big yard toward the bare trees beyond. "But I don't really care about that, Mr. Penn. I don't care. I've got a job. I'm good at selling other people houses. It pays well. And it's honest enough."

She stopped. Her tears were dried now, and she was regaining her equilibrium. She regarded him for a moment, and then grinned slightly. "Why," she asked again, "have I been telling you all this?"

Penn grinned back. "Life is short, Ruth. It's good to tell someone. And Zeyde," he said. "Remember Zeyde."

She turned back to the glass doors. A shrill electronic squeak broke the silence between them. Ruth reached inside her jacket and pulled out a beeper. "My office," she said. "Just a minute." She hurried out, to the cellular phone in her car.

Penn moved around the bed, picked up the photo of O'Connor and the Vice President from the floor, and set it back on the dresser. There were several others on the dresser, and one by one he set them up. Most he did not recognize. But in one he saw Gilbert, Ruth, and Ray Musto, all arm in arm, smiling broadly for the camera.

Her alibi was rather vague, he reflected. *And she still has a key to the house.*

He turned and picked up the St. Joseph's sweatshirt, and

94

was studying it when Ruth rushed back in, carrying her purse.

"That prospect for the colonial--he's ready to sign," she said breathlessly. "I gotta hurry." She went into the bathroom to repair her makeup.

CHAPTER SIX

one

Tuesday afternoon went just as I had hoped. By three-thirty, Jennifer's legs were wound tightly around my waist and we were gasping in rhythm, climbing together toward another climax. At exactly the wrong moment, there was a loud rapping on the carport door.

I reared up and almost fell off the bed as her grip loosened reflexively.

Catching my balance as I righted myself, I saw Jennifer's face make a near-instant transition from unguarded passion to a disheveled semblance of the detached and distant Muslim housewife's visage she presented to the outside world. I don't know what else I was expecting, but the sight was unnerving, as if she was slipping away from me, out of my hands.

I bent to grab for my pants, on the floor by the bed. "Christ," I whispered, "Who--?" Sudden dread swirled into my brain, TV images of stubbled dark figures, crowned with checkered burnooses and wielding Uzis, baying for blood revenge.

Jennifer sensed my panic, and took quiet command. Touching my lips for silence, she slipped into a bathrobe and picked up her scarf. "When I shut the door," she whispered, "open the window and get dressed. If I come back and tap twice on the door, climb out and get away. Otherwise, wait." She knotted the scarf behind her head and shut the door silently after her.

The window frame behind the partition by the desk was old and stiff with paint, but after some straining I got it to lift. A glass storm window hung outside it, fastened with simple hooks that I pulled silently from their eyes. Cold air seeped in as the bottom edge of the frame popped loose from the jamb.

I sat on the edge of the bed and fumbled for my socks. Having an escape route ready didn't make me feel much better. After all, what self-respecting band intent on taking out an infidel adulterer wouldn't have someone watching the back way?

I was just slipping on my sneakers when the door suddenly opened. Jennifer leaned against the doorway, regarding me with an ironic smile. In her hand was an envelope.

For a few seconds I was confused. Then I recognized a green Certified sticker.

"It was the mailman," she said drily, loosening the scarf. "Your substitute. The short, chubby one."

"Herman," I breathed, and looked down at the floor, smiling at myself, feeling silly at my panic. The image of Herman, rotund and sluggish, was the exact antithesis of my fevered fantasies. "Good thing I parked behind the chicken coop," I said finally.

Jennifer nodded, and tore off the end of the envelope. "No return address," she murmured. "I wonder what this is all about?"

I knew, of course. "It's--" I started.

But she was reading, not listening. The sheet, torn carefully from a recent copy of the Weekend Section of the *Washington Post,* had caught her attention. *"'The Shenandoah Chamber Music Festival,'"* she read. "In Winchester? Why did you--?"

She now looked quizzical and interested; the spectre of Jennifer as the distant orthodox housewife was fast being diluted, rinsed out of her countenance. My chest felt as if someone had loosened a vise from it.

"Yeah," I said, "at the Conservatory. It's the top chamber music event of the season, even beats the Kennedy Center." With each phrase my voice was rising and I was talking faster, hoping my words would coax her all the way back from that other identity, the one from which I was, not angrily but nonetheless necessarily, excluded.

"Tickets are pretty cheap too, considering," I hurried on, leaning over the sheet to point, "and, see, Perlman is supposed

97

to be there, and Stoltzman and this guy Bormann they say is the next Rampal. You don't get much more all-star than that.''

"When is all this happening?'' She frowned at the small print.

"It's already started,'' I said. "Nancy Reagan was at the opening, which was last weekend, thank God, some kind of fundraiser for her 'Just Say No' stuff.'' I tugged her hand down to peer at the ad. "See, we missed Stoltzman; too bad. But the Mendelssohn Octet, with Perlman, and Mozart's Flute and Harp Concerto, with Bormann, are still coming up. God, what a lineup.''

I felt her eyes on me. "And you want me to--'' she hesitated, "--go with you?''

A rush of sheepishness swept over me. The idea had seemed so right at the time, but it sounded utterly outlandish thus vocalized. "Well,'' I shrugged, "it was just a thought, really. But, well, yeah, I guess that was the idea. I mean, it was only--''

But now she was rubbing her chin and gazing toward the open window, through which the winter draft was still streaming.

Handing me the ad, she walked around the partition, to latch the storm window and shove the casement down. Then she stood there a moment, pondering the gray thatch of leafless shrub branches that I had been ready to dive into a few moments before. Staring past her, I saw there were thorns on them. I sat down on the bed again. Thank god for Herman.

"The Octet is one of my favorite pieces,'' she said quietly to the window. She turned and came toward me. "You want me to go out with you, to this concert, when?''

I stuttered. "W-well, the Mendelssohn and Mozart are tomorrow night.'' Then I noticed that she was smiling again, crookedly, mischievously. There was a glint in her eyes I hadn't seen before, the reflection of preadolescent conspiracies, the smirk of a kid about to stick her hand in the cookie jar. "It's just a thought,'' I repeated lamely.

She shook her head. "No, no,'' she protested, "it's more than a thought.'' She sat down beside me. "It's very tempting.''

"But,'' I objected, now the devil's advocate against my own foolhardy impulse, "what about the boys?''

A glance at me, her mouth now puckered in calculation. "Their aunt could keep them," she mused. "I could say I have to work a double shift; it's happened before."

"But," I persisted, "what would you wear? The scarf would give you away in a minute."

"Of course." She smiled, and pulled the scarf away, shaking her hair loose. God, I loved the look of it unbound like that. I reached out to feel it tentatively.

Her fingers closed over mine. "I'd just have to go in disguise," she mused.

"Disguised as what?" I stroked her cheek.

She laughed. "As an infidel, of course. I have regular clothes, believe it or not." She took my hand and kissed the back. "No one would recognize me in a skirt and blouse, that's for sure."

She moved her hand to my chest and gently pushed me down on the mattress. Her eyes were shining. "Perry Adams, she murmured, looming over me, "the things you think of to cheer me up. They're crazy, but they seem to work. Imagine, going out on a date with a beau, just like any other American woman. It's mad, it's totally reckless. But... for Mendelssohn and Mozart by this Bormann and Perlman, it might just be worth it." She began unbuttoning my shirt.

Her robe had fallen open and her breasts swayed into my line of sight. "You mean you'd really do it?" I was incredulous.

More obstacles swarmed into my brain: I didn't even have tickets yet; the concert could be sold out; they might not take my past-due credit card; a hundred other things could go wrong. And behind these smaller fears was an echo of the panic that had struck when Herman knocked on the door just that handful of minutes ago: What if someone did recognize her?

But these caveats faded in the glow of Jennifer's surprising enthusiasm, and the sight of her taut brown nipples.

"Will I do it?" she repeated reflectively. "I don't know. I'll have to think about it. But that comes later. Right now there's unfinished business to take care of." Her fingers pulled at my belt.

I reached to cup her breasts. "Right," I said, referring as

well to my unvoiced anxieties. "Later."

two

When Lemuel Penn's investigation came into sudden focus on Wednesday morning, he was ready for a break. After his hurried call on Ray Musto, Tuesday had been a steady succession of brushoffs, snubs and rebuffs. He had waited fruitlessly to speak to Abernathy, while Lorena flashed her silver and made excuses with increased poise. *(She's learning fast,* the watchful Sue Lee observed from beyond the partition; *the girl might make it yet.)* There was no response to several followup calls to Ray Musto. And he endured maddening telephone runarounds from the Fairfax County Police and the Postal Inspection Service.

After spending the night on a large, sagging couch on the third floor of the Quaker Committee on Congressional Concerns, Penn awoke hearing echoes of the question that had recurred so often the day before: "And who are *you* with, sir?"

It was one of the basic Washington questions, and he clearly needed a more impressive answer to it than, "A friend of Postmaster Walter Ferris," before he could get the information he was seeking. And he wasn't sure where he could find a weightier response.

He was still mulling this problem over when the break came. Fortunately the only credential he needed for it was a quarter, the price of the *Washington Post* at the Seven-Eleven around the corner, to go with the loaf of whole wheat bread and quart of nonfat milk that were the raw material for his breakfast.

Richmond Bacon Hadley, arriving early as always, thumped slowly up the stairs into the office, a newspaper under his arm, as Penn was tearing slices of bread into small pieces and dropping them into a pool of milk in a plastic bowl on an end table.

Hadley watched in silence as the younger man reached into his suit pocket, retrieved a white plastic soup spoon, and began quietly slupping the soggy chunks into his mouth.

Hadley shook his head. "I don't know how many times

100

I've seen you do this, Lem," he said. "But I'm still not used to that diet of yours."

"Simplicity, Friend, simplicity," Penn replied. "It's economical, nutritious, easy and plain."

Hadley was wiping at his eyes with his large handkerchief. "Plain is right," he declared. "It's entirely unencumbered by such worldly frills as flavor and texture." He turned to his desk, eased into the venerable wooden swivel chair, and unfolded his paper. Behind him, Penn finished his repast and followed suit.

After a moment, Hadley turned his head. "Your man is in the Metro section," he murmured over his shoulder.

"Where?" Penn asked, turning the large sheets.

"Front page."

Penn turned over a few more leaves, and sure enough, there it was: His first big break, in the third paragraph, courtesy of the journalists who had perhaps the best answer to the key question of credentials of anyone in town:

"Fairfax County police said that their search of O'Connor's house turned up reservation forms for a flight to Costa Rica today. Congressional sources confirmed that the victim was a target in an ongoing probe of defense contracting irregularities. They speculated O'Connor was planning to flee the country to escape an impending subpoena to appear before the House Government Operations Special Investigation Subcommittee. The inquiry, these sources said, is ongoing."

Penn folded the paper and looked at Hadley's back. Was it bent over the World section, he wondered, weighing the day's prospects for disarmament talks, or was his old friend momentarily and privately indulging himself elsewhere?

"Any news from Winter Haven?" he asked quietly.

Hadley chuckled, and Penn knew he had guessed right.

"Nope," the elder sighed. "The Orioles still need stronger pitching, and it doesn't look like they've found it." He tapped the paper smartly with his big hand. "But it's early in spring training."

He turned some pages. "Not much news from Geneva either. And more trouble in Beirut. What about your man in

101

Fairfax?''

"They wanted him on the Hill. That explains all the hubbub in Abernathy's office the other day. What do you know about this defense contracting investigation?''

Hadley leaned toward him. "Not much,'' he admitted. "But my friend here does.'' He pivoted back to the desk and flipped the power switch on his PC. The computer began to whir and the small screen turned amber. Numbers flashed in an upper corner as the machine awakened and stretched its electronic limbs.

"Of course, defense contractors have been robbing the public blind forever,'' Hadley went on. "But I've never seen anything like the past few years. Two of our interns spent most of the autumn entering data about the major contractors and their political connections. We should be able to learn something from their files.'' He fumbled among floppy disks in a plastic box, selected one and eased it into a slot.

"Don't think much of these gadgets,'' Penn grumbled.

"Wait a minute,'' Hadley said. "You will.''

Penn stood and moved toward the desk, peering over Hadley's shoulder as his stubby farmer's fingers picked at the beeping plastic keyboard. A list of files came up on the screen.

three

Jennifer tried half-heartedly to convert me. I guess it's one of her Muslim duties, to bring in the infidel. I also fancied it might be something of a sop to her conscience, or maybe the angel Gabriel, who seems to back up St. Peter at the Muslim gate to heaven: "Sure, Gabe, I'm sleeping with him, but these westerners are hard nuts to crack, and you have to try new evangelistic approaches....'' Doubtless Gabriel had heard it all before.

Anyway, in the course of our assignations, she gave me several pamphlets about the faith, which were clearly aimed at persuading Christians of the superiority of Muslim notions about the Bible and Jesus and whatnot.

I looked at them, but it was a tough sell. I'm your basic semi-academic secular humanist anyway. I knew this for sure last

102

year when I saw a sign outside a church in Manassas that asked, in big block letters, *"Where will YOU spend Eternity?"*

Where will I spend it? I thought. Probably the same place I earn it. If I ever do.

So arguments about whether Muhammad was a prophet in the line of Old Testament types like Ezekiel and Isaiah, and whether Jesus actually died on the cross (the Koran says no), don't really get my juices flowing.

To me it all was on about the same level as listening to Merle and Silas argue about baseball. Merle often railed against the designated hitter rule; Silas insisted it made for more interesting strategic moves by managers.

My sole contribution to this momentous discussion consisted of a single query one morning in December: "What's a designated hitter?"

They both looked at me with pity.

I shrugged apologetically and went back to casing my mail.

So as far as mission work goes, whether in sport or religion, I'm a pretty hopeless case. Jennifer seemed to sense this, and didn't press it, which was a relief.

At any rate, I soon began to understand that her own feelings were too complex for wholehearted missionary work. One afternoon she read me some Muslim love poetry, by women. This interested me a lot more than the apologetics, since language is closer to being my religion than any formal denomination.

She showed me that there are some serious feminists stirring in that world, though I gather they're up against fearsome odds, and not only the Ayatollah. Jennifer was tuned in to their work, as if the stanzas were Radio Free Islam broadcasts into an occupied country, like Khomeini's smuggled cassettes; which maybe they were.

Jennifer's favorite was an Iranian named Furugh Farrukhzad, who by Muslim standards was a real wild woman: married at sixteen, she loved poetry even more than her one child, whom she gave up to her husband at their divorce, in the early fifties, so she could be free to write. She produced several books of passionate verse, had lovers, was denounced as a slut and a pagan, then died young and alone, in her early thirties.

Furugh reminded me a bit of Judy Garland, except her most ardent fans weren't gay men but women such as Jennifer, who looked from the outside like loyal daughters of orthodoxy, but were churning inside with who knows what kinds of subversive thoughts and impulses.

I don't know how a religion like Islam gets changed; but reading Furugh and watching Jennifer, I began to wonder if they and their unarmed veiled sisters might succeed where armies of Christian Crusaders had failed.

four

Jennifer ducked quickly into my wagon on Wednesday night. It was already dark, yet she hurried as if to evade some watcher hidden in the bushes. But there was a brazen air to her movements, too, and she reminded me of Furugh, or what I imagine a rebel Islamic woman poet might look like: quite modestly dressed, really, but almost stylish in khaki-colored slacks and long-sleeved white shirt, medium dangly earrings and a subdued maroon silk scarf at her neck.

Her hair shimmered, parted down the middle and brushed straight back. It looked so sexy it was almost indecent; my twinge of jealousy at this brazen display brought me up short. Can it be, I thought, that I'm learning to see her a bit the way a Muslim male would? Was that a good idea? I doubted it.

She buckled the seat belt and turned her face to me, tossing the dark blond hair aside with a motion at once defiant and defensive. "Well?" she said.

"You're stunning," I answered sincerely. "You'll never be recognized."

"By whom?" she said.

I edged the wagon from her driveway onto the street. "You know. Anybody. Not even your husband's relatives."

She threw her head back and laughed. "Not those relatives," she yelped. "They're all totally Americanized. Hell-bent on learning to pass."

The bravado was comforting, but I still wasn't sure.

104

"Enough so they might like classical music?"

"Oh, please," she giggled. Try Willie Nelson."

five

She was mistaken, though she didn't find it out until after the conservatory's star players stars had sawed through a spare, demanding Ginastera quartet, and then Perlman and Company had romped brilliantly through the Mendelssohn.

The concert was in the Conservatory chapel, a cozy rounded hall with high, dusky red brick walls. Long multicolored banners hung from one side, and an abstract stained glass window, colors indistinct with the night behind it, was embedded in the bricks on the other. We were in the balcony, front row, close enough to see the sweat glistening on the fiddlers' foreheads.

The sound rose around us like the aroma from a glorious garden. It was fabulous, heady. When the eight players crashed to the finale of the Mendelssohn and my hands reflexively moved to applaud, I realized I had been holding my breath for what seemed like minutes.

Jennifer seemed to be loving it as much as I was. She stopped clapping long enough to give me a radiant smile and squeeze my hand. "I can't wait for the Mozart," she shouted over the din.

Then everyone around us was up and moving to the stairs and intermission. In the semicircular lobby, smokers headed for the doors and drinkers took aim at the bars set up at both ends. Jennifer nodded toward the ladies room and disappeared in the crowd.

I pushed toward the bar and was surprised, as no doubt were the hard-core drinkers in the line, to find that the featured refreshments were local potables--Shenandoah Valley wines, and in nods to the school's vaguely Methodist heritage and the town's principal export, sparkling apple cider.

I didn't mind. The cider would work for my Muslim teetotaler date, and I'd go along for the ride. Balancing two fizzing plastic goblets, I navigated carefully toward the opposite

105

wall and the ladies'.

After five minutes standing there, sipping demurely at the cider, she hadn't appeared and I was getting antsy.

The lights blinked a first warning for the second half. The crowd started shuffling toward the entrances, crowding around the stairway. The outside doors clanked inward as the stream of addicts returned, trailing toxic smoke. Three of them pushed noisily past me, laughing raucously at some unheard outside joke.

I resented them. Which one was hiding Jennifer from me? The fat one with the big bald spot? The thin one with the bow tie and the mustache? The hip-looking one in the leather blazer and the beard? I knew they had her. But where? Stuffed into a softpack?

Then she was there, somehow at the far end of the lobby, stepping from behind a seven-foot high plastic potted palm. When she knew I'd seen her, she jerked her head once toward the outside door, and then slipped past another laggard smoker through it. Even from that distance, in just that second, the fear in her widened eyes was engraved on my mind.

A fat lady coming through the door bumped into me, and a golden stream of cider splashed on the edge of her dress. She squawked and recoiled, brushing convulsively at the spots. I didn't stop to apologize.

six

Jennifer was crouched behind my car, shivering. All her bravado had vanished.

"He saw me," she shuddered, when we were inside. "My God, he saw me."

"Who?" I insisted, steering the car toward the access road with one hand, and trying to put my other arm around her shoulders.

"No!" she snapped, pushing my arm away. "Drive with both hands." She took a long breath. "My brother-in-law."

"What?" I hissed. "Mr. Willie Nelson fan? What the hell-?"

She wrung her hands. "I don't know. I swear, he wouldn't know Mozart from Mickey Mouse. I can't imagine why he was there."

"You sure he saw you?"

She thought a moment, then shook her head. "No, I guess I'm not," she sighed. "I think so, though. He looked right at me. But he was listening to some woman, and maybe I didn't register."

We were at a red light, waiting to turn east onto Highway 50 toward Middleburg. Something came to me. "When was the last time he saw you, you know, with your clothes on--minus the scarf?"

She stifled a snicker. "Come to think of it, I'm not sure he ever did. That's a thought, isn't it?" Her breathing was slowing a little; I hoped she was starting to relax.

The light blinked green. "Wanna go back?" I asked.

She stiffened. "No," she sighed. "I couldn't."

I figured as much, and turned onto the highway. A few hundred yards further it went over Interstate 81, headed northeast to Pennsylvania and southwest to Tennessee.

"I was really looking forward to the Mozart, though." She sounded wistful as another red light stopped us on the overpass. She reached up and delicately unhooked the gold earrings, dropping them into the jacket of her pantsuit.

We waited in silence, and I glanced at the rear view mirror. Lights pulled up behind us, and others crept along the right side. I tapped out the rhythm of the Mendelssohn's opening allegro on the steering wheel.

What if he had recognized Jennifer? Would he come after her? Maybe, just to be on the safe side, it would be a good idea to find a different way home. Do something unexpected, make sure nobody was after us.

The left turn arrow flashed on the empty lane down to the interstate. I counted to three, then floored it. Jennifer gasped and grabbed at the armrest as the car squealed across the vacant lane and down the ramp.

Jennifer's mouth dropped open. "What--?"

"Just a little evasive action," I said, in what I imagined

107

was a suave, James Bond tone. "Nothing to worry about, my dear. Nothing at all."

But it was a lie. In the rearview I saw clearly that the second car back, something sleek and Japanese-looking, had also jumped the lane and followed us onto the interstate.

seven

Walter Ferris was even more put off by Lemuel Penn's diet than was Richmond Bacon Hadley. In fact, he was downright unnerved when his companion pulled a wrinkled plastic bag from the capacious pocket of his suit jacket, retrieved two rumpled slices of whole wheat bread from it, and started tearing them into pieces, which he dropped into a bowl.

If I didn't need Penn's help, Ferris thought, I wouldn't put up with this. And when Penn lifted a glass of milk and started pouring it over the mess, Ferris could not keep quiet.

"Couldn't you at least get a salad?" he muttered over his sirloin tips. The postmaster warily surveyed the late dinner crowd in the steakhouse dining room, hoping no one he knew was watching. "People will think we're weird."

"All right," Penn conceded, "if it eases thy mind, Walter." He stood and headed for the salad bar.

"That's better," Ferris allowed when Penn returned with a plate of tomato chunks and cucumber slices. The postmaster forked a steak fry, dunked it in ketchup, and waved the fork at Penn. "This," he pronounced, "is real American food." He chewed contentedly. "Now what were you saying about campaign contributions?"

"It's somewhat complicated," Penn said. "But it starts with the fact that Gilbert O'Connor was a sub-subcontractor. Most of his work came ultimately from United General."

"Newport News?" Ferris asked, biting into the beef.

Penn nodded. "Second largest shipbuilding company down there. They used to do mainly submarines, aircraft carriers, the real big ships. But now they're heavily into support systems for Star Wars."

"Star Wars?" Ferris was mildly incredulous. "But that's

108

all missiles, outer space."

"Perhaps so," Penn agreed, "but the missiles have to fall somewhere, and the ocean is the preferred place. In any case, Star Wars is getting so much money thrown at it, nobody wants to be left out."

"I get it," Ferris acknowledged. He grimaced as Penn dipped a cucumber wedge in the milk. "But so what?"

"With that much money flowing that fast, opportunities for waste and corruption abound. And United General's record the past few years is worse than most. Cost overruns, delays, accidents."

Ferris sneered. "So what else is new? Contractors were ripping off George Washington at Valley Forge."

"Of course, thee's right. But they've also been investigated off and on ever since. Many a Congressman has made a reputation that way. And Richard Abernathy hopes to do the same thing."

"Bully for him." Sirloin tips demolished, Ferris stifled a belch, picked up a toothpick and began gnawing it. "Lock 'em all up, 'far as I'm concerned. Even if they have to put 'em up in our Valley. Make for a better class of criminals than the usual dope dealers and rapists."

"Possibly," Penn conceded. "But while Abernathy was hot after Gilbert O'Connor, he doesn't seem to have noticed what's happening with United General itself."

"The sonofabitch," Ferris swore. "What's his angle?"

"My sources suspect it's the great god ambition," Penn said. "Abernathy wants to run for the Senate next year. For that he needs money and votes. Especially votes in the Tidewater, at the other end of the state from his home base in the Valley."

"As in Newport News. Makes sense," Ferris said. "There and Norfolk are the biggest metro area in Virginia. I put in for a postmaster's job over there once. Bigger station, paid lots more." Ferris stifled another belch. "But who needed that much more aggravation?" He did not mention that he hadn't been offered the post.

Penn nodded. "And it is no surprise that United General runs one of the richest political action committees in the state.

Abernathy has already collected $50,000 from them.''

Ferris looked up from the cigarette he was lighting, squinting into the curl of smoke. "Don't tell me," he grunted. "O'Connor was supposed to take the fall for United General, while Abernathy let them get away and he collected his money and votes." He coughed. "Christ, what a world. If my job wasn't in jeopardy, I'd almost feel sorry for the dead guy."

"Really?" Penn needled. "Walter, who's the liberal now?" Then he shook his head. "I'm for law and order here. O'Connor didn't have to steal money from the taxpayers. But thee's right. It's an old question, 'Why does God let the wicked live and prosper?'"

Ferris regarded him steadily. "I believe you're bucking to be a genuine wise guy in your old age, Lem."

Penn ignored the sardonic tone. "Not me," he said, "but Job had it right. Ecclesiastes also."

"More stuff from the Good Book?" Ferris's guard was up. "Remember my rule: No sermons. No lectures either. Save that for your adult class in Washington. And anyway, all this maybe explains why O'Connor wanted to skip out, but what's it got to do with his getting killed? He's no good to Abernathy's reputation in a coffin. And none of this tells me how to get my neck off the chopping block."

"Fear not, friend," Penn said. "I remember thy rule about lectures. But there's one other verse I can't get out of my head: 'With all thy getting, get understanding.' That's Proverbs. And I don't have it yet. You're right: there's more to understanding how Abernathy and O'Connor and United General all fit together in this than we know. Something's missing. Maybe a lot is missing."

"Missing? Something that can get me in the clear?"

Penn shrugged. "I don't know. Maybe. So I think tomorrow I better climb back up the Hill and try to fill in some blanks." He gazed vaguely toward the salad bar. "Perhaps," he mused, "the committee would be the best place to start."

"Good idea," Ferris said. He tilted his chair back and narrowed one eyelid. "But while you're up there, do me one favor will you?"

110

"Sure," Penn said. What?"
"Don't pack a lunch."

eight

One exit north of Winchester on I-81, I knew, was Route 7. It was the alternate route east, bypassing Leesburg and circling back toward Fairfax. I raced toward it, pedal to the metal, weaving around cars and trucks like some kind of madman.

I was half excited, and entirely terrified, by the speed. My workdays are spent creeping along the shoulder at ten miles an hour. Sitting in mid-seat and steering one-handed so as to reach mailboxes through the open passenger window are about as reckless as I normally get.

Jennifer swayed stiffly beside me, one hand on the armrest and the other clutching my arm.

The other car stayed right with us, too. It was, I decided after a few nervous glances at the mirror, probably a Toyota. A Maxima. Something fast as hell, anyway.

It closed in as I slowed for the exit. Turning east on Seven, I was relieved to see no taillights ahead. "No traffic," I murmured. "Thank god." As I floored it again, Jennifer clutched at me harder, and turned her head to look back.

We flashed past a fruit stand and a succession of large gray historical markers. The markers were barely a blur in the dark, but I knew what they said. Along this route in September, 1864, General Phil Sheridan led a Union army across Opequon Creek and through a narrow canyon in a successful assault on Rebel-occupied Winchester.

Sheridan's success was a close affair. His troops got stuck trying to cross the creek, and then strung out in the canyon. Jubal Early's grey Confederate troops almost trapped them there. Almost, but not quite.

Now we were retracing Sheridan's route backwards, toward a narrow bridge over the creek and then back through the canyon. A few miles further, a causeway rose high above the course of the Shendandoah, where the river entered the last lap of its journey to the Potomac and the sea.

111

As the causeway came into view, the Toyota closed in again. I realized with a shudder that unless the guy had some kind of Uzi to empty into us, his best bet was to try to run us off the road on the approach to the low bridge.

Into the river in the dark. How deep was it there? I had no idea. Hell, at this speed a few inches was deep enough.

Then a tractor trailer with a ten-foot high red apple painted on the side trundled into view from a side road, barely hesitated at the highway, and turned out in front of us.

Jennifer gasped, and I reflexively hit the brake. Then I saw our chance.

"Hang on," I yelled at her, hit the horn and jerked my foot back to the accelerator.

The truck driver must have heard me, because the truck swerved to the right as I passed, as if afraid I was going to hit him. Then as his wheels began to sink into the shoulder he swerved back to the left, and oversteered just enough to send the trailer into a jackknife, blocking three of the four lanes as the driver fought to keep the rig from tipping over.

We were on the causeway, above the darkened river, when Jennifer, straining to see behind us, gasped, "he stopped. He had to. He almost hit the truck."

I nodded, but something else had caught my eye. Just beyond the causeway, a roadsign bore the name Aldie and an arrow pointing to the right down a county road. Aldie was right near Middleburg, and Middleburg was on Highway Fifty. That was the other way, our original route, back to Fairfax.

I slowed and eased onto the backroad, grateful when a stand of tall trees closed behind us.

"Where are you going?" Jennifer's voice was small and frightened.

"Home," I said, trying to sound reassuring. "Right home. It's okay now, Jen, honey."

She didn't answer. We rode in silence for several miles. With no one in pursuit, I began to notice the countryside. A half moon gave the gentle slopes of the Blue Ridge a benign, almost protective look, reinforced by the scattered sparkle of house lights.

I could feel myself slowly relaxing. "It's pretty country," I said aloud.

Jennifer didn't answer. But her breathing had slowed too, and she loosed her grip on my arm.

By the time we reached Aldie, I felt safer, almost jaunty. A little Mendelssohn, a little chase over the Shenandoah--just what the doctor ordered to banish the winter doldrums. Right?

But there was something I wanted to know. Needed to know. The sign for Highway Fifty came in view, at a red light.

"Jennifer," I said, as we waited for the green, "you okay?"

She glanced at me and nodded quickly.

I hesitated. The signal facing the highway turned yellow, then red. "Jen," I said, letting up on the brake, "who is this brother-in-law of yours?" In case, I was thinking, he comes after me again.

I realized she had moved away, toward the door. A pale green washed over the lines of her face as we passed under the light, and her eyes were pools of shadow.

"It's Ray," she said quietly. "Ray Musto. He runs a security guard--"

"Oh, Jesus." My sharp intake of breath interrupted her. "What?"

"I think I know him."

nine

"Rahman Mustafa Mahmood. That was his name back home. He changed it when he was naturalized. Said Musto sounded more American."

Jennifer's gaze was now fixed on a van that had edged in ahead of us, and she seemed to be talking to someone in its back seat. "He has only the trace of an accent, and people think he's Italian, or maybe Greek. He likes that, so he lets them."

She paused. "But what is he to you?"

I felt as if a number two mailbag, the one that holds seventy pounds of mail, was draped across my shoulders. "Gilbert O'Connor owned the company he runs."

113

Now she looked at me, sharply. Her eyebrows were crowding together, and I could see she was processing this data as rapidly as I was.

"Wait a minute," she said, "do you mean--?"

I shrugged. "I don't know what I mean. This is as new to me as it is to you. But suppose he wasn't even looking for you. What if he was after me? What if Ray Musto is the one who shot O'Connor, and then at me, and thought it was time to finish the job."

Jennifer looked ahead again, then brought her hands up to cover her face. "No," she said through her fingers. "No, that couldn't be. Ray was never like that. He--" she trailed off.

We rode in silence for more miles. The hills were behind us now; Chantilly and the far suburbs were coming in view. To the north a big airliner angled up from the tree line, taking off from Dulles International Airport. We were back in civilization.

Maybe--" Jennifer started, then stopped.

"'Maybe' what?" I coaxed.

"Maybe," she said, "this--this expedition wasn't such a good idea." I hardly recognized her voice. It was low, and sounded bone-tired. "I don't know, Perry. You've been very good to me. Good for me. But--" she trailed off again.

"But what?" I demanded. "What, Jen? Look at me. Please."

She let her hands fall. I expected her eyes to be wet, but they were dry, and deep. "But maybe we pushed it too far."

"No," I protested. "No, Jen, we didn't push it too far. He did. We just wanted to enjoy some good music together. What's so wrong about that?"

She didn't answer. We rode in silence all the way into Fairfax, then turned at the courthouse, past Fairfax South and to her place.

When I pulled up the drive to the door she touched my hand, whispered "Good night," and was out of the car.

When she turned on the inside light, the glare framed her in the doorway for a split second. I wanted to call out to her then.

But I didn't, and the door closed behind her.

114

CHAPTER SEVEN

one

The Chief Clerk of the House Government Operations Special Investigations Subcommittee was a Mrs. Jensen. She was middle-aged, with graying hair and what looked like chubby twin granddaughters.

But neither Mrs. Jensen nor the granddaughters were anywhere around her desk in the subcommittee's large, white-paneled outer office on the second floor of the Longworth House Office Building. Lemuel Penn read the clerk's name on a black plastic nameplate on her desk; he learned of the granddaughters by turning around a ceramic-framed photo next to the nameplate. He wrote down the name and his deductions in a reporter's notebook, and looked around the offices. It was lunch hour on Thursday, and there were no committee staff in view. The place seemed deserted.

Penn went back into the hallway, thinking vaguely of trying to raise someone at Abernathy's office in the Rayburn Building next door. Perhaps the young Lorena, she of the flashing braces, could find someone to help him. Or maybe one of the officers standing guard downstairs.

At the street entrance he went up to the Capitol policeman seated behind another large desk, sipping from an oversize styrofoam coffee cup and keeping a wary eye on the metal detector which framed the doorway.

"Excuse me, officer, er," Penn squinted at the nametag on his breast pocket-- "Hanrahan, my name is Lemuel Penn, and I wonder if thee--"

He stopped, flustered. Hanrahan, he thought. The name Lorena called out in Abernathy's office when O'Connor's body was found. A sergeant; the three stripes on his sleeves confirmed

115

it.

"What can I do for you?" the officer was saying. His expression was somber but not unfriendly. Penn asked about the empty subcommittee office.

The policeman nodded. His large, lined face became more thoughtful. "Yes, Mrs. Jensen is out today. She's getting chemotherapy treatments; breast cancer." He regarded his coffee cup for a long moment. "They're a real ordeal," he said, and took a sip. "She's lost weight, her hair is mostly gone, she wears scarves all the time. But they say she'll pull through." He pursed his lips. "Let's hope they're right."

He glanced back up at Penn. "What is it you need up there?"

"I wanted to read some hearing transcripts," Penn said. "Last year's shipyard oversight hearings."

"Well, that shouldn't be a problem," Hanrahan said. "I can let you into the reading room, and somebody'll be back soon enough."

Hanrahan called to an officer on the other side of the entryway. "Frank, I'm taking this gentlemen up to 324. Keep an eye on things." He reached into a drawer and retrieved a large ring of keys, then stood up. "Come on."

Walking behind Hanrahan into the elevator, Penn recognized the logo on the keyring swinging in the policeman's large hand. The doors closed and they stared silently at their reflections in the door's polished brass panels.

"You know," Hanrahan said, still thoughtful, "Mrs. Jensen--Susie to us--she gets paid pretty big bucks here, she does, considering she never finished high school. Worked her way up from receptionist to Chief Clerk. Sometimes you wonder what the point is."

The elevator bumped lightly and the shiny door slid open. Penn stepped out first, turned to Hanrahan and murmured, "Well, thee knows what they say: *Et in omne possesione tua adquire prudentiam.'*"

Hanrahan laughed hollowly and shook the keyring. "'With all your getting, get wisdom,'" he echoed. "Proverbs Four. Hell of a way to get it, though." As they turned into the

116

doorway at 324, he abruptly swung around to face the visitor. His expression now held a challenge. "For her, it's more like, *'Eo quod in multa sapientia multa sit indignatio.'*" He regarded Penn steadily.

Penn returned his gaze. "'For in much wisdom is much grief'", he repeated. "Ecclesiastes. I can see why thee would remember that verse."

"You study to be a priest too?" Hanrahan asked.

"No," Penn said. "But I had Latin in school, and particularly liked Proverbs and Ecclesiastes in the Vulgate. They seemed somehow more eloquent in Latin, especially about the futility of everyday activities and pretensions. Like what thee just cited. And of course, *'Omnia tempus habent....'*"

Hanrahan nodded. "'To everything there is a season,'" he translated. "And now is the winter of her discontent." He turned and jingled the keys in the lock on the reading room door. "But that's Shakespeare. More or less."

The large door swung open on a cramped room, walls lined with thick, library bound volumes of Subcommittee hearings and reports. On a polished oak table sat a stack of newer hearings, still in the standard tan paper covers.

"Well," Hanrahan said, "if this is the season for you to read about shipyard hearings, Mr. Penn, you came to the right place."

He turned toward the door. "If nobody's back when you're done," he added, "just let me know downstairs."

"Is it all right," Penn wondered, "for me to be in here by myself? I mean, aren't there sensitive documents around? Government secrets?"

Hanrahan waved a dismissive hand. "Nah, those are all locked in a safe in the back." He smirked. "This stuff is strictly *'Vanitas, Vanitatum'*. Read your fill, Mr. Penn."

Penn grinned back. "*'Omnes vanitatum,'*" he finished the line, "'Vanity of vanity, all is vanity'. I always liked that one better in the King's English." He scanned the laden shelves warily. "But to tell the truth, this place looks more to me like *'faciendi plures libros nullus est finis.'*"

Hanrahan laughed aloud at this. "'Of the making of

117

books there is no end.'" You got that right. I'll bet old Ecclesiastes worked for the Zion Government Operations Committee. Enjoy yourself, Mr. Penn, if that's the right word."

"I'm sure I will."

Penn was leaning over his notebook, absorbed in a thick set of hearings when he heard someone come into the room. He looked around and found a trim, serious-looking young man staring past him at the book.

"Excuse me, is that one of the shipyard oversight hearings?" the young man asked.

Penn nodded. "Volume Two."

"Ah," the young man said. His expression clearly showed that it was the one he wanted. "We're all out of copies," he said apologetically, "except for the bound ones here."

"I won't be much longer," Penn said, "er--"

"Phil Gibb," the young man answered. He extended his hand. "I'm on the staff here. Just bring it back to my desk when you're ready."

Penn shook his hand. "Certainly," he said.

Hanrahan was back at his station at the street entrance, nursing another large cup of coffee, when Penn emerged from the elevator, a sheaf of papers folded into his notebook.

"Find what you needed?" the sergeant asked as the older man passed the desk.

Penn paused and shrugged. "Not much more than *'nihil sub sole novum,'*" he said.

Hanrahan grinned. "'There's nothing new under the sun' all right. That's pretty good, Mr. P. You should have been a Catholic. You'd have made a good Jesuit."

Penn raised an ironic eyebrow. "Sergeant," he said, "I'll take that as a compliment."

Upstairs an hour later, Phil Gibb peered at a passage in the thick book of hearings, then picked up his telephone. He pressed the keys and waited. He spoke without preamble.

"I think I've found it. Show you tonight." He hung up.

two

Richmond Bacon Hadley looked up from the notebook, the sheets covered with Penn's careful script, and tapped at the paper reflectively. Then he rubbed the crease on the copies from the transcripts where they had been folded.

"The pattern is clear enough, Lem," he said. "But it's nothing new, and I'm not sure what it tells us."

Penn sighed heavily. He didn't want to agree, but he knew Hadley was right. "What I didn't realize before was just how cold-blooded Abernathy has been about that crane accident last year. Three men were killed when it collapsed; two others paralyzed. And the OSHA report clearly implied that it was United that had been negligent. But he kept turning the questions about it away from United General to the manufacturer, in Minnesota. Isn't that--?"

Hadley's big, callused hands were up, as if to push away the barrage of words. "I know, I know," he said. "It's shameful. But it's nothing obviously corrupt. Members protect their own. Especially the ambitious ones, which is most of them. Always have." He lifted a newspaper clipping. "And he covered himself. Got the U.S. Attorney to come up with a couple of indictments."

"Yeah," Penn sighed. "I saw it. The crane contractors, out of Baltimore." He ran one hand through his thinning hair. "I hate all this, Rich. It isn't Christian to feel this way, but I just hate it."

"It isn't Christian," Hadley affirmed. "But I won't tell the Overseers just yet."

"Isn't there some way to--?"

"Around here they have an expression," Hadley said: "'Paybacks are hell.' But we've never gotten into that business. Our motto has to be, "'Vengeance is mine,'' saith the Lord.'" He took a breath. "The Lord's--and the voters of the Commonwealth of Virginia."

Penn pointed to another set of papers balanced precariously on his lap. "The PAC reports say that Abernathy got another $25,000 from United's PAC just last month."

119

Hadley sighed and gazed out the window at the whitewashed sepulcher that was the Capitol dome. "If wanting to run for the Senate was a crime, Lem, you'd have him dead-bang. But what any of this has to do with that fellow getting shot out in Fairfax is beyond me. Anybody with Abernathy would want him alive, playing his part as a small-fry sacrificial lamb."

Hadley shook his head, and borrowed his antique Quaker address. "If thee asks me, Friend, thee'd better start seeking elsewhere. Way doesn't seem to be opening here."

Penn looked thoughtful as Hadley lifted the papers with one hand, swiveled to face his desk, and dropped them in a pile next to the computer.

He picked up a pink slip. "Oh, yes," he said over his shoulder, "there was a call for you yesterday from Ellen Phyle, the clerk down at Washington Friends Meeting. Something about a lecture?"

"Right," Penn said absently. "Sunday. The Adult Class."

"No," Hadley said, "They want to change it to Saturday. Some potluck's already set up and their speaker fell through."

"That shouldn't be a problem," Penn said. "I'll be back by then."

"Back from where?"

"Easton, I think."

"Easton Maryland?" Hadley asked. "Nice town. Third Haven Meeting's there. Oldest house of worship on the Eastern Shore. George Fox preached in it, 1672, I think."

"Yes," Penn mused. "I've been there. But I was thinking of visiting another church institution this time."

Hadley turned toward him. "Which is that?"

"St. Joseph's Military Academy. Gilbert O'Connor's alma mater. Maybe the Romans can help me out."

"You think they can come up with some leads?"

"Maybe," Penn said. "But maybe something else too."

Something in his friend's tone made Hadley swivel back around. "What's that?"

Penn was staring out the window again. "The military part," he said evenly. "Perhaps they can teach an old Quaker

120

something about vengeance.''

But Penn found no military instruction waiting in Easton Saturday morning. In fact, once he parked his Valiant, walked past a new redbrick gymnasium and approached the older administration building at St. Joseph's Military Academy, he found no one waiting for him at all but a statue of the school's patron, on a pedestal in front of the entrance.

The granite saint Joseph was gazing devoutly skyward, and held nothing more martial than a bouquet of long-stemmed plaster lilies. His pacific piety completely spoiled the effect of the facade behind him, which rose on either side in halfhearted concrete imitations of fortress turrets. A Spanish-American war-era cannon guarded a flagpole on the Saint's right flank, but didn't do much to redeem the scene; its mouth was plugged shut and crocuses were blooming around each of its wide-spoked wheels.

Penn walked past the statue, up the wide stone steps, and pushed through arched oak doors. Inside, a sign pointed to the right, down a long polished hallway to the office.

There Penn found an aging bald priest, in a long brown cassock, seated behind a counter, intent on an old book held open in his hands. Penn could read the title, just above gnarled fingers: *Introduction to Mariology.* Penn asked softly, ''Father Cletus?''

The priest looked up, revealing thick glasses above a scraggly grey beard. He squinted. ''Mr. Penn?''

''Yes.'' Penn extended his hand. This gesture seemed to disconcert the priest. ''Oh,'' he exclaimed, ''excuse me,'' and stood up. He closed the book, turned and hurried to a bookcase against the far wall, sandals slap-slapping softly against stockinged feet as he moved. He carefully slid the volume into a slot between two other venerable-looking tomes. As he returned his thin arms seemed to flutter in their hanging brown sleeves, and Penn realized that his cassock was tied at the waist with a length of rope, into which was interweaved a dark-beaded rosary.

121

A Franciscan, Penn thought as the priest finally took his waiting hand. Reading a book on the Roman's Goddess cult, no less. So much for this school as a stronghold of militarism.

"It's very good of thee to see me on a weekend, Father," he said aloud.

"Oh," said Father Cletus, "perfectly all right, perfectly all right. Everyone is gone, as I told you on the phone. Father Ludger, our Dean, has taken them off to the archbishop's youth convention in Baltimore. I just rattle around in here anyway. Just rattle around. A little company doesn't hurt." He scratched at his lined forehead with a thin finger. "Now what was it you wanted to know about? Something to with scholarships. Do you have a son who is interested in applying to St. Joseph's?"

Penn felt himself reddening. "Err, no. Actually, I was wondering about the scholarship funds donated by one of your prominent alumni, Mr. Gilbert O'Connor. The late Mr. O'Connor."

"Ooohh." At this name Father Cletus's mouth formed into a whiskery circle. His finger dropped from his forehead to his belt, and Penn heard the muffled rattle of the rosary beads. "Yes. A terrible thing, poor man. Terrible thing. We've been saying novenas for his soul all week. He was a great benefactor to the school."

He abruptly stood up and returned to the bookshelf. "You might find the yearbooks for his class interesting," he said, dumping several oversized volumes with shiny embossed covers on the counter. "Did you know Mr. O'Connor?"

"Not personally," Penn said. "Actually, I'm involved in an investigation of his death, and the question of his gifts could be material to it, though of course it's all a matter of routine at this point."

The circle of Father Cletus's mouth had clamped abruptly into a thin line at the word "investigation," and he was squinting again. Penn wondered if the cleric was trying to discover a police badge of some sort on Penn's suit jacket, and if he was familiar with that deflating Washington question about who this stranger represented.

But evidently he wasn't. "I see," he responded neutrally.

"What exactly did you want to, uh, want to know about these gifts?"

"Well, say, how many gifts there were and what size, during the past three years?"

Behind the glasses the priest's brows crowded together. "I'm not sure I'm allowed to tell you that, Mr. Penn. Donor information is very confidential, you know. very confidential."

"I understand," Penn nodded. "But we already know some of it, from records found in his house after the, uh, tragedy. He was one of your largest donors in recent years, wasn't he?"

"Ah, the largest," the priest said. "That's no secret, sure enough. No secret at all. Gave most of the money for our new gymnasium himself, he did, and pointed us toward those who gave the rest. Then he doubled our scholarship endowment in one stroke."

He pondered a moment. "Let me get the file," he said. "This is something better handled by Father Ludger. But there may be some items I can talk about."

He came back from the inner office with a thick manila file folder. He laid it on the counter a few feet from Penn, opened it and began sifting through the sheets of paper. After examining three or four, he shook his head slowly. "Oh, Mr. Penn," he murmured without looking up, "I don't think there's much here that I could show you. Not without talking to Father Ludger, and I expect he'd say we'd need permission from Mr. O'Connor's family."

Penn did his best to look cooperative and understanding. "I see," he began, and then a telephone rang in the office behind the priest. The ring was unusual, almost like a buzzer.

Father Cletus immediately looked up and snapped the file folder shut. "Oh dear," he said, "that's the emergency number. Oh dear, an emergency." He scurried through the doorway, the folder under his arm.

"Hello," Penn heard him say. "Oh, Yes, Father. Yes? Anderson? The sophomore? Didn't bring it? Right, I'll find it and have it ready here. Yes, thank you."

He came back and went to the end of the counter, lifting a section to let himself past it. "One of our cadets," he said breathlessly, "an epileptic, forgot his medication and has had a seizure. Had--"

"--a seizure," Penn completed the repetition.

The priest glanced sharply at him. Penn was impassive. "Father Thomas is on his way to pick it up, if I can find it."

He pulled up short at the door, remembering something, a finger rising to his cheek. "Probably in his locker, downstairs," he murmured. "I'll need the combination." He whirled, went back into the office, and emerged with a sheet covered, Penn could see, with numbers. "I should just be a few minutes," he said to Penn. "Just--"

"--A few minutes."

Penn stood listening to the slap of his sandals down the long hallway. As the sounds faded, he considered a moment, then moved swiftly: past the still-lifted section of counter, and behind it into the office. There under a large print of an ever-watchful St. Joseph was a large desk with a telephone, and next to it the file folder. Penn lifted the cover and riffled quickly through the sheets.

When Father Cletus came padding back down the hall, Penn was back where he had been, paging through a yearbook. The priest hurried in carrying a plastic bottle with a pharmacy's label. He placed the bottle on the counter and contemplated it.

"This has happened before with Anderson," he said. "We're beginning to suspect he rather enjoys the fuss and attention. Rather enjoys it. But we can't take the chance of his hurting himself." He glanced at a wristwatch. "Father Thomas should be here shortly."

He watched Penn turning the yearbook pages, and his attention seemed to shift back to the visitor with difficulty. "Was there anything--" he said, but Penn raised a hand.

"There is one thing," Penn said. "It looks here as if Gilbert O'Connor and George Hanrahan were pretty close." He pointed to a picture. "Here they are on the basketball team." He turned several pages. "Then here on the drill team. Did you know them?"

The priest blinked. "I don't really--"

"Never mind, Father," Penn soothed, "I can see this

124

isn't a good time. I'll take this matter up with Father Ludger next week. I hope your student will be all right.''

"Yes," the priest agreed. "All right. Here, I'll walk out with you.''

Penn drove through Easton to the quiet, wooded block of South Washington Street where Third Haven Meeting stood. The new meetinghouse was large and substantial; beyond it was a small cemetery and the smaller, wooden structure in whose bare interior the founder of Quakerism, George Fox had once preached. The caretaker let Penn in, and he sat in the chilly room on a narrow bench polished only by time while meditating on his visit to St. Joseph's.

Although the Puritans were among the fiercest enemies of Fox and early Quakerism, Penn reflected, Fox's cultural outlook was almost identical to theirs. St. Joseph's was not especially ornate as Roman establishments went, but Fox would have railed at the pictures, the statue of St. Joseph, all of it.

Fox much preferred the austerity, the starkness of meetinghouses like this one: bare benches, bare walls, bare religion; take the money spent on those popish frills and fripperies, he would have thundered, and spend it on the starving poor.

Fox the social radical would have been equally offended, Penn realized, by the school's curriculum. Study war no more, he would have demanded. Learn the arts of peace. Not that the place had seemed particularly warlike that morning, under the stewardship of the birdlike Father Cletus.

But what would Fox have made, Penn wondered, of the letters in the folder, describing a series of large gifts to such a place. Not the mere fact of them, but the pattern; especially the pattern of the letters conveying the gifts. So much money, and not only from O'Connor, but from others he had solicited. There had not been time to read them closely, yet all the letters he had seen were signed, not by Gilbert O'Connor, but on his behalf, by Barbara Keene. It looked as if she had handled the entire transactions, with O'Connor doing little more than signing the checks, and showing up to accept the awards.

125

Penn thought back, to their conversation in the Roy Rogers near O'Connor's office. What was it she had said? Something about, "There was plenty of work, all right. The past couple years I could hardly keep up with it." Keene had protested against the insinuations that she was O'Connor's lover. But clearly she was something more to him than simply a secretary.

Penn rubbed his chin, and realized he was cold. He stood up and headed out of the small spartan meetinghouse toward his car.

Just how much more, he wondered, was that young woman to O'Connor and his operation?

four

Jennifer didn't answer her phone all day Friday. By Saturday morning, with still no answer, I was frantic. So there was nothing to do but to go by her place and see what the hell was going on. But I couldn't just drive up and start asking questions, especially if her kids were around. So I had to have an excuse, a cover.

Which meant I had to have some mail. And that meant making a trip to South Fairfax. At least I had a reason for that, because Friday had been payday and there should be a paycheck for me there.

But going out also meant maybe putting myself in the sights of whoever had chased us from Winchester. I figured I was safe in my apartment, a needle in the haystack of South Arlington, with my car pulled around the back off the street. I should probably just sit tight. It was a fine idea, smart. Except that I was going nuts.

So before leaving I walked around the side of the house and peered cautiously up and down the street, feeling foolish as this revealed no more than the usual suburban weekend scene. Then I drove way out of my way, down Interstate 395 to the Beltway, then down I-95 to Lorton and up Silverbrook Road, coming in the back way to the station.

Lucky for me, Ferris wasn't there, it being a weekend.

But Herman Corson was, casing Route 66. He was alone in the back; Merle and the other carriers were already on the street. This wasn't a surprise: Herman wasn't the fastest at casing anyway, and being new to the route was slowing him down further.

But nervous as he was, Herman also knew the RCR's secret, the unspoken truth which I had also figured out after a few weeks without being told: Regular rural carriers are paid a flat salary, so the faster they get finished, the sooner they can go home. But RCRs are paid by the hour, to fill gaps. So if an RCR shows up regularly and sober, he doesn't have to rush; if the Postal Service had a faster way to get the routes covered, they'd have done without us long ago.

Still, there are other things in life than work, even for an RCR, and I could tell Herman was anxious to get on with it. "Hey, Herman, what's happening?" I said, coming up to the case, "How's it going? Here, let me help you out a bit. I'm getting stir-crazy at home."

"Sure, Perry," he said, relief showing in his broad face.

I grabbed a handful of letters and began slipping them into the slots. "We got paychecks?" I chatted. "Mine'll have to stretch awhile I guess."

"Yeah, that sure was a mess," he said sympathetically.

I shrugged. "It'll get straightened out," I said smoothly, as if murders were a routine occurrence in my life. I said. I waved the bundle of mail in the direction of Silas at the desk. "You go get the accountables," I urged, "I'll do this, and route your parcels."

"Sure, Perry, thanks," he said.

As soon as his back was turned, I reached up into the second row of slots, marked Fox Run Shoals, and pulled out everything for 3603: two envelopes and a magazine in Arabic. Then as I laid out the parcels on the floor in the order of the route, I saw one with Jennifer's address. It was small, looked like a free sample of something.

No matter; it and the envelopes fit easily inside my flannel shirt. I grabbed a yellow slip from the supply I kept in an empty slot in the bottom row, and stuffed it in my pocket. Then

127

I headed for Ferris's office, where Andy was filling in for Ferris as acting supervisor, or 204B, to get my paycheck.

"Parcels are done," I called as I headed out toward the door. "Watch out when you get to Kasabians. There's a parcel for them, and those Nazi dogs'll rip your throat out if they get a chance."

"Okay, Perry, thanks. I will," Herman said gratefully.

This was more conversation than we'd had in a month, and probably more than we'd have in another six weeks, if I ever got back to work. If Merle had been there, with his loathing for Herman's putative homosexuality, I probably wouldn't have been able to do it. I felt a twinge of guilt at being so shamelessly manipulative, but didn't pause to consider it; I was feeling desperate.

five

And after all that, it was hardly worth the trouble. No shoes were lined up outside Jennifer's door. There was no sign of the goat. My knocks went unanswered. I had given up and was getting back in the wagon when an old Honda pulled up the drive, and out stepped the woman in the red scarf. I grabbed the parcel, yellow slip attached, jumped out and thrust it at her.

"This is for Mrs. Mahmood," I said. "Is she here?" The woman shook her head, took my pen and signed the slip, impassive as ever.

"When will she be back?" I persisted.

Now she looked directly at me, for perhaps the first time. Her thick lips moved. "Gone," she said. She waved a hand and wrinkled her nose, as if waving off a fly, or dispersing a foul order. "Gone," she repeated loudly. "Away."

I could see that nothing less than a refined and extended round of torture would extract any more information from her. I sighed and got back in the wagon. I felt her eyes on me as I pulled down the driveway, and that reminded me that somewhere out here somebody else was looking for me too, with murder on their mind.

six

Driving back past the station, I saw that Merle's jeep was in the lot and pulled in. He was finishing some late casing for Monday, and seemed glad to see me.

I needed a friendly face too. "Merle," I said, "when you're finished here, could we get a cup of coffee somewhere?"

"Sure, he said, "how 'bout the Pizza Hut. I ain't had lunch yet. Lemme buy you a slice."

Over the pepperoni I told him about the chase, and with some trepidation, confessed to being with Jennifer. His eyes widened when I explained her relationship to Ray Musto.

"Sheee-it!" he exclaimed, pushing back his Legion cap for further emphasis. Then he leered appreciatively. "Getting some half-Arab nookie, eh? Goddam, Perry, you got more gumption than I figgered. And he tried to run you off the road? The bastard. What'll it be next?"

"That's what I'm afraid of," I said. "Guess I better watch my back."

Merle threw a crust onto his plate. "Well, hell, man, that ain't no way to live. You can't just crawl in a hole and hide. Let's turn the tables and follow him."

"But follow who?" I demanded.

"Musto, who else?" Merle insisted. "He's your best bet, and if it ain't him, it'll drive whoever it really is crazy, throw 'em off stride. Maybe they'll make a mistake."

"But I don't know Musto," I objected. "I wouldn't recognize him."

Merle pondered a minute. "Well, I know 'im," he said. "Useta carry mail there, saw 'im lotsa times." He picked up another slice of pizza. "What the hell," he proposed, "let's use my car. Musto won't recognize it." He took a bite.

"You sure?" I asked. "You don't need my trouble. I've been shot at and chased this week already."

Merle laughed, and the smell of garlic wafted across the table. "Why not?" he said. "I got nothin' better to do. The Superbowl's over, and baseball season ain't for another six weeks. I had fun gettin' into old O'Connor's place t'other night. I could

129

use a little more excitement.''

He hunched forward in his seat, the idea pumping him up. ''Look, I know his car. It's a gray BMW, and his license is one o' them vanity plates: OnGard2. And if I recollect right, he lives not far from the office.''

Merle abruptly stood up and pulled his cap down into a determined angle. ''Hell, let's go,'' he declared. ''We'll show 'em.'' He tossed a dollar on the table for a tip, grabbed another slice, and headed for the door.

CHAPTER EIGHT

one

Merle's car was a big Ford, which sounded souped up. He called it the Lucky Lady, and it must have been, because we were a block away from Glenn's Ferry when I spotted a grey BMW coming towards us with the telltale plate: OnGard2.

The window glass was tinted and I couldn't see who was driving. I tapped Merle's arm, and when he saw what I was pointing at, he swerved into the lot of the Roy Rogers, and turned around.

"Hell," he shouted, "this is almost too easy."

"Maybe," I answered. "If he's our guy."

Half an hour later we were waiting for a light by the Tyson's Corner shopping center. The BMW was two cars ahead of us. When the light changed it pulled out and drove straight for the mall, heading into one of the multi-level parking garages.

Merle stopped outside the garage. "Well, I'm glad I had that extra slice of pizza," he said. "Guess we got a stakeout to do here. Like my MP days. Better relax, Perry. Take a nap if you want, then you can spell me. We could be here awhile."

But we weren't. I was just dozing off when Merle shook me and started the Ford's engine. "Here 'e comes," he said, and I caught a glimpse of the BMW sliding past us. Merle turned into the garage entrance, backed out and squealed off in pursuit.

We saw Musto turn onto Leesburg Pike and headed west, but we were several cars behind. "Don't lose 'im!" I called, opening the window and leaning out to keep his car in view.

Traffic was thick on the Pike, as usual, but Merle wove expertly among the cars, and we closed on him. Just beyond the toll road to Dulles Airport, we saw the BMW's lights signal for

131

a turn. "He's headed for the hotel," Merle commented. "'E's got somebody with 'im, too."

Sure enough, the BMW made the left into a long access road lined with new young trees, their smooth and slender branches yearning toward spring. At its end the road became a flat ellipse in front of the Fairfax Courtyard Suites Hotel. We followed the BMW around the ellipse and into the garage beneath the hotel. When we found it, in a space on the lower level, I looked the other way and saw a couple, their backs toward us, just entering the elevator to the lobby. Merle slid into a space nearby.

"If that's them," I said, contemplating the blank grey of the concrete wall, "this time I think we will be here awhile."

"Yeh," Merle agreed. "This time I'll nap first. Keep an eye out for 'em."

two

But I wasn't cut out for surveillance duty, because again it was Merle who shook me awake. "Dammit, Perry," he chided, "good thing we weren't on the front line, you'd get us both kilt."

"Sorry." I sat up and rubbed my eyes, frowning at the wall, getting my bearings. "How long have we been here?"

He consulted his watch. "Over an hour. Lucky for us the BMW's still there. But the hell with this. Let's go inside, find a place to watch the elevator with something cool in our hands." He opened the door.

The hotel was built around a large rectangular courtyard, with the suites rising for seven floors on all four sides, along balconies that overlooked a huge central lounge. Behind the elevators was the lobby at one end of the ground floor. A bar and buffet were at the other end, with round white tables and big potted ferns scattered in between. The lobby elevators were glass-walled on the lounge side.

"Perfect setup for us," Merle commented, surveying the scene. He turned toward the bar. "Let's get a beer."

Over the first Budweiser, Merle began cogitating aloud. "So Musto picked up a lady friend at Tyson's and headed here. I'll bet he's been here before with her."

132

"A secret life," I said. "Wonder if he's married. Jennifer didn't say."

Merle took a long pull of his beer. "What I wonder," he said, "is where was Mr. Musto last Monday, when his boss was getting perforated? What sort of alibi does he have? You don't s'pose--"

He stopped, looked toward the elevators, and pursed his lips in the inverted U shape that betokened intense concentration. "I got an idea," he said after a moment. "Where's the house phones?"

I followed him out toward the lobby. The house phones were around a corner, next to a bank of pay phones. Merle picked one up.

When the operator answered, he screwed up his features and started talking in what seemed to me like an utterly phony Hispanic accent. "Esscuse me, senora, but I gotta room service order here for, uh, Meester Moosetoe, only I no can reada the room number. I theenk it's maybe six oh three, or even five oh eight, the keetchen people they don't write no good, you know? Can you help me a leetle beet, senora, por favor pleeese?"

I rolled my eyes, but he was listening and ignored me. Then he grinned. "Oh gracias, thank you senora, muchas gracias, I be there right away."

He hung up and gave me a thumb up. "Now for step two." He moved to the next house phone and picked it up. "Front desk, please," he said to the operator.

My eyebrows rose. This time his voice was lower, more poised, his country accent almost completely suppressed. "Pardon me, madam, this is Mr. Musto in 708. I was here earlier this week, and I've been reexamining my receipt, and it looks to me as though the check-in time is incorrect, and I was erroneously charged for a extra day. What do your records say? Yes, I'll wait."

He winked slowly at me. "Oh, really? Twelve forty-five on Monday? Yes, that's much closer to what I remember. Perhaps it's a misprint on the receipt. Yes, I'll bring it by before I check out, just to make sure everything is straightened out."

He hung up and punched me playfully in the arm. "You

133

see that?'' he crowed. "Two in a row. Damn, I'm good." He pursed his lips again. "Could be I'm mistaken," he mused, "but our man might have an alibi. Seems he was here about the time old O'Connor bought the farm. That makes two visits in one week. Wonder what he sees in this place?"

"Or whom?" I mused. Something began to surface in my memory. "Wait a minute--didn't that secretary, Barbara what's-her-name, tell us that Musto was at some naval research place all that day?"

Merle considered this. "Not exactly," he recalled. "I remember she said he called in and *told* her that was where he was. He coulda been somewhere else. Like bumpin' off his boss."

"Or here," I quipped, "doing the courtyard bump."

Merle frowned. "Speakin' o' which, we better get back to where we can see the elevators." He strode toward the lounge. "Besides, this problem calls for another beer."

Waiting at the bar, I mulled over the information. If Musto checked in here at twelve forty-five on Monday, that would have been around the time I was at O'Connor's. So he would be just about in the clear. It must be a half hour drive from Bluebird Lane to here. More if the traffic was bad, which it often was.

The barmaid brought our beers and I turned to follow Merle to a table. The lounge was almost deserted: this was the slack time between the last of the lunch crowd and the first of the happy hour horde.

"But if he was here," I said as we walked, "then chances are he didn't shoot O'Connor. And if he didn't do that, why would he have wanted to chase me out of Winchester?"

"I figure it this way," Merle said, "if he recognized Jennifer, that mighta been enough." He set the beer down on a table and pulled out a chair.

"But wouldn't that--" I began, reaching for a chair myself.

That was when the barmaid screamed, there was a crash behind me, and a flying piece of crockery, or maybe an ashtray, clipped my right ear. I dived reflexively past my chair, wondering in a flash if the shooter had sneaked up on us.

134

But Merle was up and shouting. "Jesus Christ! *Jesus Christ!*"

I scrambled to my feet, feeling dazed, and put a hand to my ear, expecting it to come off in my hand. But there was only a small smear of blood on my fingers. I realized that I wasn't really hurt. I felt a big relieved grin stretch my cheeks.

"I'm okay," I said vaguely to Merle.

But Merle wasn't there. He was somewhere behind me, still shouting, and the barmaid was still screaming.

I whirled and staggered and grabbed at the table to steady myself. Merle came into focus pushing his way among several upturned round tables, fumbling at something dark and inert. Still holding my ear, I stumbled toward him, and realized that the inert something was a man in a dark suit. In my daze, it seemed as if Merle was wrestling with him. But as I got closer I saw that he was pulling him loose from an overturned chair, and it was hard because the man's body seemed completely limp and broken. And Merle was still shouting.

"Somebody call a goddam ambulance! For chrissake, the guy might still be alive." With a final yank Merle got the chair out of the way, and then rolled the man over.

I leaned against a nearby table, my hand still at my ear, and focussed on the man's face. It was thin, with a mustache. And he had a bow tie, at the base of a neck which was bent the wrong way.

The combination was familiar. I had seen them in the lobby of the chapel at Winchester. It had to be Ray Musto.

three

The barmaid had stopped screaming. I heard more tables and chairs being shoved aside and looked up. A couple of security guards were hurrying towards us. Merle straightened up and held his hands out, keeping them at a distance.

"Don't touch him," he warned. "I think there's still a pulse, but there's gotta be a lotta internal injuries. Let the med techs move him."

One of the security guards was talking low into a walkie

talkie. "Did you see it?" the other one asked me.

I shook my head. "The waitress," I mumbled. "At the bar. She screamed. She must have seen it." I squinted up at the tiers of balconies. "I think he fell." The security guard turned back toward Musto.

From outside I heard the descending shriek of an ambulance, and someone was pulling at my sleeve.

It was Merle. "C'mere," he urged, pulling me toward the lobby end of the lounge. I followed obediently.

When we were back by the house phones, out of sight of the lounge, he suddenly shoved me up against the wall and shook me hard, his hand gripping my shoulders so tightly it hurt.

"Perry!" he hissed. "Snap the hell out of it. Jesus, we gotta move."

The shaking was bringing me back into focus. "Something hit me," I said.

"It was a freakin ashtray," he snapped, glancing at my ear. "You'll live. Unlike Musto in there. Now come on, we gotta move."

"Where?" I asked, feeling confused.

Merle leaned in close to my left ear. "To the room, dammit. I got a key." He lifted a hand, the palm toward me, and I could see flat against it one of the new credit card type room keys, with little holes in it.

"It was in his pocket," he whispered fiercely. "I got it before the security cops came. 708, remember? We gotta check it out before the cops get here. Come on, wake up and follow me. Christ." He hurried toward the elevator.

four

Room 708 was empty, and looked almost undisturbed. Almost, but not quite: the spread on one of the two beds was rumpled, but it hadn't been slept in. Pillows were piled together at the head end, and a towel was draped over the foot. A room service tray with a nearly empty wine carafe and two glasses sat on the small round table by the window. One glass showed faint lipstick stains on the rim when Merle held it up to the light, a

136

washcloth wrapped around his hand to avoid leaving prints.

I sensed something else too: an aroma in the room, faint, indefinable, yet in unmistakable harmony with the rest: the odor of recent sex.

Merle recognized it too. "Looks like he had one last hump before his one last jump."

Being there was bringing me back into focus again. "But who was it with? And was she the pusher?"

"My guess is she was," Merle said. "She sure got the hell outta here fast enough."

He put the glass down, carefully. "Let's take one quick look around this place and then we gotta make like hockey players and get the puck outta here." He tossed me another washcloth. "Don't touch anything solid with your bare fingers." Lifting the mattress on the rumpled bed, he looked between it and the box springs. Then he leaned down to peer under the bed.

I searched under the other bed. Nothing. Then I opened all the desk drawers, and picked up the Gideon Bible. Flipping through its pages, a business card fell out.

"Merle," I called out.

He was moving toward the door. "Show it to me in the car," he said. "We gotta get movin'."

Through the elevator's glass walls I saw that his MP's sense of timing had been on the money. Two cops and a security guard were leaning over the seventh floor balcony, tracing the path of Musto's dive to his death. Another minute and they would have seen us come out of the room.

In the car, back on Leesburg Pike, I fished the card from my pocket and handed it to him at a stoplight.

"'New Century Realty,'" he read. "'Ruth Solomon.'"

"Who's that?" I asked.

CHAPTER NINE

one

"In the Wisdom books and passages of the Hebrew Bible," Lemuel Penn declared confidently, "one of the most important themes is the dialectic, indeed the struggle, between Wisdom as good advice--what could be called an ancient Israelite Dress for Success formula--and Wisdom as meditation on mystery, especially the mystery of entrenched, unpunished evil, particularly evil in high places."

He paused to survey the group. The audience of forty or so, spread along the dark oaken benches of the Washington Friends Meetinghouse, was listening respectfully, faces upturned, all eyes fixed on him but those few whose lids were closed.

"This struggle," he continued, "is what I want to talk about tonight."

Despite their postures of attention, Penn wasn't sure they were really with him, or rather with his subject. These liberal Quakers, he knew, were unfailingly polite to visitors. But given their training in focussed quiet for silence-based worship meetings, it could sometimes be awfully hard to tell when they were enraptured, and when they were on the verge of dozing off.

Still, Penn was confident he knew the text, and the subject had long fascinated him, so he hoped his enthusiasm would be contagious. Of course, he faced the added complication of a potluck supper being assembled in the common room downstairs. Thus Penn was having to vie for their attention with a mix of aromas floating up the stairwell: he had already identified beef stew, and something distinctly casserole-ish, probably with lots of pasta and cheese. Lasagna, most likely.

As distracting as these scents were for him, given his austere preferences in cuisine, Penn figured they must be much

138

more so for his listeners. Fortunately, he was only expected to introduce the topic at this point. The main presentation, and discussion, would come after dinner.

Penn paused to clear his throat and turn over a sheet of notes. The door at the side entrance to the meeting room banged quietly, and he glanced to his right.

The light was dim there, but in the doorway he made out two figures who didn't fit with the scene before him. Urban Quaker couture was a study in middle class motley, but this new pair was more rough-cut, what you'd see at a garage or on the line at a factory. They seemed familiar, but he couldn't place them, and the uncertainty broke his concentration.

"Err, this struggle," Penn said, "is most sharply posed in the, uh, confrontation between the book of Proverbs on one side, and Ecclesiastes along with Job on the other."

He paused to rub his forehead. It was damp. "In Proverbs," he continued, "virtue and shrewdness are much the same, and always lead to prosperity and honor as well as God's favor. The somber, skeptical book of Ecclesiastes mounts a direct, harsh challenge to this whole worldview. This challenge is echoed and deepened by the story of Job."

He looked furtively toward the door again. The newcomers were just standing there, not moving to a bench. And was one of them signaling to him?

"We, uh, also find this conflict expressed in several of the, ah, Psalms," he continued. "In fact, Psalm 89 may be the best summary statement of the conflict that we have."

Now he remembered; of course: Henderson, the mailman from Fairfax, whose brother played ball for Staunton. And the younger one, Adams. What were they doing here? And Henderson was definitely signaling to him.

"Er, we will read this psalm as a way into this conflict, he said, "and then look at some other related texts."

He paused again to reach for his Bible and readjust his notes, and as he did so picked up a definite rustle from the benches. Then he knew that between the smells from downstairs and the distraction from the doorway, he'd lost whatever hold he'd had on these Friends.

139

Time to regroup. Penn moved his hand away from the Bible. "But you've been awfully patient with me, Friends, considering how hungry you must be. So I think we'll read this psalm after dinner."

A polite chuckle marked the release of tension, and after the ritual moment of silent grace, the group broke up and streamed through the side door, past the two intruders and toward the stairs and the food below.

two

"Let me get this straight, Perry." Penn was still struggling with disbelief. "You think Musto tried to kill you the other night--and now he's dead? And Ruth Solomon is involved?"

He wouldn't have credited any of it, but when Adams produced the business card from New Century Realty, he realized they must be telling the truth. He turned the card between his fingers and saw some numbers in pencil on the back. "What's this?" he queried.

Perry peered at the digits. "I didn't notice them before," he said. "Could be a phone number; first three digits are 304. Dunno what it's for."

Penn stared at the numbers a moment longer, then returned the card to the younger man. Abruptly his mind switched to another question. "How did you find me?"

"I called Mr. Ferris," Merle volunteered. "He told us to get to you right away, and said you was at some Quaker outfit in town. It wasn't this one--some committee on the Hill. Didn't figger anybody'd be there on a Saturday, but a fella answered on about the twentieth ring, and he sent us right here."

That would be Hadley, Penn surmised, working on a weekend again.

"What else did he say to do?" Penn was already planning to call Ferris himself at the first opportunity.

"Said he'd call the postal inspectors, and we'd need to talk to them, soon as he could set it up."

That sounded right. "What about Ruth--Mrs. Solomon?"

140

Penn's mind was racing, wondering about how to find her, and what she would have to say about this.

"No answer at either number on the card," Merle said. Then his eyes shifted, and his nostrils flared. He pushed back his American Legion cap. "That beef stew I smell?" he asked with frank interest.

The remark brought Penn back to the present. "Of course," he said. "Come on down, both of you, and let's get you each a plate. You must be famished."

At the bottom of the stairs a pay telephone hung on the wall in the corridor. Perry veered toward it. "You go ahead," he called. "I wanna check my messages. I'll be right there."

But when he came to their table a few moments later, he seemed agitated and had no interest in food. After nodding and shrugging restlessly at a few more of Penn's questions. he interrupted.

"Look," he said to Merle, "I just got an urgent message about somethin' I gotta do. I'll take the Metro from Dupont Circle back to Arlington, and I'll talk to you tomorrow."

"Hey, buddy, slow down," Merle protested. "I won't be that long. It's a long ride that way, and there's no need. And this is great stew."

"Don't you want to eat something first?" Penn echoed. But the young man was shaking his head, and holding his hands up in a defensive gesture.

"No, no thanks," he almost shouted, "it can't wait. I gotta go." And before either of the other two could repeat their pleas, he was trotting up the stairs and out of their sight.

"Jeez, what got into him?" Merle queried. "I wonder what he heard that sent him off in such a hurry?"

Penn stuck his fork in a chunk of bread that, in a concession to the indulgent potluck spirit, he had consented to douse with gravy from the stew. "I hope," he said slowly, "it didn't have anything to do with money."

three

I was halfway back to Arlington before I remembered that

141

my wagon was at the station. But it was my luck that when I got off the Metro there was a Metrobus loading up for a concert in the Patriot Center at George Mason University. From the campus it was still a two mile walk to South Fairfax, headed into a fresh breeze that sent the wind chill cutting through my jacket.

I didn't care. My ears were burning and my nose was running, but once I got into a steady walking pace the rest of my body felt warm enough. And my goal was clear: get to the car, warm up in it somewhere in the dark, wipe my nose on the stash of paper napkins in the glove box, and be at Ferris's Store by ten. That was what the message on my answering machine said.

The message from Jennifer.

four

I was in the lot, my ears thawed out and my nose wiped clean, with time to spare. I sat with my lights off and the radio on low, running the engine intermittently to keep warm, and waited.

There wasn't much traffic. At twenty after ten a car drove slowly past the store, turned the corner and then pulled into the entrance on the other end of the lot. It stopped by the gas tanks, and the flashers went on: one, two three. The car then drove slowly out onto Fox Run Shoals. I turned the ignition and followed it.

There's a small cluster of houses in the woods adjoining the store's lot, which you enter on Shamrock Lane a quarter mile down. It's on Merle's route, but I've covered it a few times. It's one of the older developments in South Fairfax, so it lacks a pretentious name and a big sign at the entrance. But there's lots of space between the houses, thickly grown shrubbery everywhere, and a secluded cul de sac at either end of its course.

The car ahead, which I now saw was a Honda, turned into Shamrock, and I followed closely, guessing right that it was aiming for the cul de sac at the far end, which was furthest into the woods.

When we stopped I opened my door to the biting wind, and quickly got into the Honda on the passenger side.

142

The dome light flashed on as I opened the Honda's door; she had forgotten to turn it off. In the momentary brightness I saw that she had on the scarf and the shapeless tan coat. Her eyes still glinted grey-green, but the old original sadness was back in them. The door thunked shut and she was an oval silhouette.

I was shaking, and not only from cold. I didn't know what to say to her, what to do. Once I had helped banish the sadness from those eyes. Now they seemed miles away, and I felt helpless.

She broke the silence, speaking slowly and quietly. "Perry, I'm sorry I disappeared. I was afraid, for you as well as myself and the boys. And I needed to think."

"To think?" I asked. "What about?" The anger in my voice surprised me. "I-I'm sorry," I retreated. "I have no right to demand anything from you. But I've been afraid too. Then today, when Ray--"

I heard her gasp, and involuntarily reached for her hand. "My god," I said as her fingers closed tightly on mine, "I'm sorry, didn't you--?"

"It was on the radio." Her voice cracked and gave way to a sob.

My other hand felt for her cheek under the scarf, and then she was in my arms, sobbing against my shoulder. Back where we started, I thought grimly. "Oh, Jen," I breathed, and reached to pull the scarf up far enough to reach her forehead with a kiss.

After a few minutes she pulled back far enough to be able to talk, her voice a near whisper. "I was so afraid he was coming to get you, or me, after the concert. And now that he's dead, I'm even more afraid. For you, for me, for all of us. Even Rashid."

"Rashid?" I was a little incredulous. Her husband was several thousand miles away from this week's madness. If Beirut wasn't safe, at least it had different dangers.

"I know it's silly," she said. "But if it wasn't Ray who was after us, then who was it? It could be anybody. Somebody from there, come here to get me. Or you."

"Wait a minute," I objected. "That's been my line. You were the one who always said such talk just echoed western media

143

stereotypes. What happened?''

"What do you think?'' she wailed. "This week.''

She stiffened in my arms. "I've been praying a lot these past few days,'' she went on. "It may sound silly to a secularist like you, but it's what I needed to do.'' She wiped at her eyes. "Not just for forgiveness for--for us. I also wanted to know Allah's will for me.''

I could sense where she was headed. "Allah's will? About Beirut?''

"Yes,'' she breathed. "Something important is happening there. I'm not sure I can say what, exactly. But I think it's more important to be there, facing enemies that are real, than here waiting for the boys to be sucked away from me by Nintendo and rock music.''

She sniffled, and looked sheepish. "And then, a wife should be at her husband's side. I haven't been a very good wife these last weeks, but there it is.''

"Okay,'' I said, "agreed on that. But what about a wife being under her mother-in-law's thumb?''

She leaned against the seat, staring through the windshield into the darkness. "Yes,'' she whispered, "what about that?''

"And your music?'' I pressed. "What has Allah told you about that?''

Her head turned sharply. "Don't mock me!'' Then she sighed. "But I still don't know what to do. For a true Muslim the path of duty and the will of Allah are the same. So I guess I'm still a westerner, at least partly. I want a personal message.''

I felt myself starting to shake again. "Well then,'' I blurted, "I'll give you a personal message, if not from God, at least from a real live human.''

I fumbled for her hands. "Don't go, Jen. Stay here. Stay here with me. We can be safe, we'll hide somewhere and start over if we have to. Bring the boys, too. They'll like me. I think Hassan does already. He acted like it when we talked at the door those times. And, hell, America's a big country. We could find someplace to be happy, where I could cheer you up whenever you were sad. We could--'' now my voice went husky, "--we could learn to love each other. I already love you.''

144

I could feel her eyes, searching me, burning into me. Her fingers touched my cheek, and stayed there. "I've thought the same thing," she whispered. "I don't know if I could do it. But I've been wanting to."

Then she kissed me. I tugged at her scarf, wanting it loose so I could get my fingers in her hair. She pressed against me, her lips parted and her tongue probing mine. My right hand slid down from her cheek to her neck, then across her coat to the swell of her breast. I groped for the buttons, wanting to get inside, into the warmth of her. Jennifer's breathing was coming faster.

Then I had an idea. I pulled my hand away and felt for the radio buttons. This was a moment that needed some music, and I was sure she'd have it set on WETA.

My fingers closed on the power knob, turned it clockwise, felt it click on.

I had guessed completely right, and completely wrong.

The station was there all right, loud too. But it was just starting the full orchestral version of Barber's Adagio for Strings.

the Adagio is a fine piece--if you need music for a funeral or a soundtrack for a war movie. It's about as far from erotic as you can get. She jumped at the chords and shrank away from them and me.

I snapped the button off. Only a few bars of the music had come into our little sanctuary, but they had pierced the intimacy like needles into a balloon. I tried to enfold her again, but she pulled back firmly.

"Perry," she said, "I do want you, very much. But I need to sort this all out, and I have to do it on my own." She was silent a moment. Then she added, in a tired voice, "I need to go now. If the boys wake up, they'll be terrified to find me gone."

She touched my cheek again. "Please."

I tried to snatch one final kiss, but she turned her head and my lips only grazed her cheek.

"Will you wait here a few minutes after I leave?" she asked, as I was getting out. I nodded.

145

While I waited, I turned my radio on. The Adagio was just finishing up, and it seemed eerily appropriate now. Then a soft purr of news came on.

Well let's see, my life was a mess, but according to the State Department, plans for a summit between Reagan and Gorbachev were going swimmingly, according to the State Department. As, for that matter was the countdown for the Space Shuttle Challenger's teacher in space mission; in a cheery sound bite, Christa McAuliffe, the anointed New Hampshire pedagogue, repeated how anxious she was to blast off. The latest government reports were saying that inflation is down, unemployment is down, but the deficit is up.

I started the car, and let out the emergency brake. Damn inflation. Jennifer was gone, I wouldn't be following her. Now I remembered that I was hungry.

And another American, the announcer calmly added, had been taken hostage in a Beirut shootout. A professor of Physics, kidnapped near the American University. Two killed, several wounded, the professor's condition was unknown. In a written statement, President Reagan condemned the kidnapping, and said the U.S. would not tolerate any more terrorism against Americans.

"Yeah, sure," I yelled at the radio. "Hit 'em hard, Ronnie; drop a photo opportunity on them. And then if they don't say uncle, go all the way, blast 'em with your three by five cards."

The announcer talked blandly on, about the next round of the NCAA college basketball tournament. At the corner of Shamrock and Fox Run Shoals, I was tempted to drive past 3903, to see if Jennifer had gone back to the house.

But I didn't, turning instead toward the station, wondering whether Jennifer had heard the news as she drove wherever she was going. Rashid was teaching English, she had said. And he probably wasn't even an American citizen yet. Did the snatchers distinguish between green cards and citizen's papers? When would his turn come? I bet she was asking these questions too.

146

It didn't come today. A bittersweet sigh of relief leaked out of me. That was a relief. I didn't want to get to Jennifer by seeing Rashid dead in Beirut.

Or did I?

All right, so the thought *had* occurred to me. For about ten seconds.

After all, there was enough killing going on around here. Too much, actually. I didn't want any more of it in my life, even from that distance.

And I didn't need a personal message from Allah to figure that out.

CHAPTER TEN

one

The Keyes View Inn is set back from Highway Nine, just over the West Virginia border, about an hour northwest of Tyson's Corner. From the driveway it looks like a rambling victorian pile, with a wide veranda and Queen Anne towers at all four corners.

On the other side, the side facing out over the slope of the Blue Ridge, the windows were bigger, the furniture more contemporary but thickly upholstered in subdued colors. The place was quiet, insulated.

From the panoramic windows of the Inn's quietly well-appointed restaurant, Lemuel Penn had a clear view through Keyes Gap, down the shoulder of the foothills, to where the Shenandoah river joined with the Potomac below Harpers Ferry.

Except for the smog, which was a regular feature of the vista nowadays, it was a spectacular panorama. But Penn glanced toward the window only occasionally. Instead, he sat in a corner of the big room, nursed a cup of herb tea and kept watch on the young woman cashier. Or rather, he watched the restaurant entrance which opened on the lobby a little beyond where she stood, smiling at customers and efficiently ringing up their checks for the Keyes View's famous, expansive Sunday brunch.

Penn had been sitting there more than two hours. He was on his third cup of chamomile, and he guessed the waitress was beginning to wonder about him. For that matter, he was also beginning to wonder whether he had spent the morning allowing himself to be gulled. He could have gone to Quaker meeting that morning in Washington, or out this way at Goose Creek or Hopewell, rather than driving up dun leafless hillsides to this upper middle class hideaway.

148

But at a quarter to one, a woman in a dark pantsuit pushed through the doors from the lobby, and he relaxed. The woman surveyed the restaurant, spotted him, and made her way to his table. Penn stood as she approached, but she waved away his courtliness.

"You're a good detective, Mr. Penn," she said, after glancing at the menu and ordering cappucino. There were crescents of sleeplessness under her eyes. "It didn't take you long to find me."

Penn demurred. "You weren't that well hidden, Ruth. Leaving the Inn's number on your card was the first break, and when there was no Musto or Solomon registered, I tried O'Connor. And there you were."

She smiled feebly, and he caught another glimpse of Liza Minelli. "If you hadn't said, 'is it thee,' when you called, I'd have just hung up and made a run for it," she declared. "I was going to go somewhere else tonight anyway." She sighed. "I guess the CIA won't hire me anytime soon, huh?"

A couple in Sunday church clothes came from the brunch line and headed in their direction. "Amanda, don't run," called the father to a sullen-faced girl of about seven. He was carrying a loaded plate in each hand; his wife followed behind, a sleeping infant in her arms.

Amanda ignored her father and came up to the corner of the big window, about a foot from Ruth's ear. her brown hair was brushed back and held with a pink plastic barrette. Her dress was frilly, pink and flowered. Penn watched her lean toward the glass, stick her tongue against it, puff out her cheeks and breathe loudly, watching a small circle of condensation forming above her nose.

"Amanda!" cried her mother. "Stop that! Come and sit down right now!"

The woman's anger jarred the baby awake. It began to whimper. Amanda ignored her parents, continued breathing her circles, and started singing a wordless children's tune which sounded vaguely familiar to Penn.

"Oh god," Ruth groaned. "Not Sesame Street. Can we get out of here?"

149

She stood up, clutching the wine-colored cloth napkin. Not waiting for his nod, she led Penn out of the restaurant and through the lobby, to a quiet lounge at the other end, where two thick armchairs overlooked another, smaller slice of the Valley scene. She sank into one of the two chairs, glanced indifferently at the scenery, then faced Penn squarely.

"Listen," she said, "I didn't kill Ray. I don't care how it looks." Her gaze faltered. "Why would I want to do something like that?" Her voice was sinking as she spoke. "He was one of the only friends I have. Had." Her gaze wandered back to the window.

"All right," Penn replied, "does thee know who did it?"

She shook her head, and smoothed her short dark hair. "No. But I think I may know why he was killed."

Penn waited.

"He-he called me on Friday, and said he'd figured out who'd killed Gil, and why, and he had proof. He said he'd bring it and show it to me on Saturday."

"And did he?"

"Yes--well, not exactly. He started to." Her voice faltered.

"But first--?"

She faced the window again, then covered her eyes with the napkin. She sighed heavily. "Okay, okay," she murmured. "But first, he wanted to make love."

He could barely hear her whisper. "Just like last Monday?" he asked, as gently as he could. "At about the time when Gilbert was shot?"

She looked sharply up at him. Her mascara was smudged with tears. "I felt like such a slut when I heard." She made a disgusted face. "At least it was an alibi. But now that's gone too."

"How long had...this been going on?" Penn kept his voice low, his tone coaxing rather than inquisitorial.

"A year or so." She sighed again. "I suppose it was mainly an affair of convenience. You know--two lonely people comforting each other. But he was gentle with me. He didn't seem as driven as Gil was. Though maybe he was, in a different

150

way. I don't know. He took me places. He even read the Bible to me.''

"The Bible?''

A wistful look. "The Song of Songs. That's how my card got into the book on Monday. You wouldn't expect it, but it's very romantic. *'Set me as a seal upon your heart....'''*

"I know,'' Penn said. "Chapter eight.''

She peered at him quizzically. "Why do I keep having conversations like this with you, Mr. Penn?''

"Call me zeyde.'' Penn gave her what he hoped was a grandfatherly smile. "Where did Musto take thee last? Winchester?

Her eyes widened. "God, have you been following me all week?'' She shivered. "Yes, he took me to a concert. How did you know?''

"Just a guess,'' Penn's eyes were evasive. "I had a friend at the concert.''

"It was wonderful music,'' she said. "Gil never had time for those things, not after he really caught the fever. Except a couple times at the Kennedy Center, as part of some fundraiser. And he had season tickets to the Redskins, but only went once a year or so.''

"Did he know about thee and Musto?''

"I don't think so.'' She shrugged. "But what if he did? Hell, we're divorced. I'm single, yippee. He may have suspected.''

Now she was twisting the napkin in her hands. "If he did, he probably didn't care. He was too busy.'' Her eyes dropped. "That's not an easy thing to admit, though. It doesn't do a lot for a woman's self esteem.''

"What?''

"Losing your husband to a dollar bill. Though he did have his bimbos too, at least now and then. And probably Barbara in the office.''

She was silent a moment.

"What did Musto show thee?''

"That's the crazy part,'' she said. "Nothing, really. All he showed me was a little envelope with a registered mail seal on

151

it. There couldn't have been much in it. But before he got around to opening it, after we--afterward, the phone rang. He picked it up and listened for a minute. Whoever it was upset him, because he said he had to go meet somebody at the bar downstairs. He got dressed and left, said he'd be right back.''

Her eyes filled again. "That's all." Her voice was husky, broken. "Then he was gone."

She sobbed quietly. "Mr. Penn, I'm scared. Whoever did it is after me too, I know it."

"Maybe," Penn said. He leaned over to pat her hand. "But thee can come with me. I know where thee will be safe." He was thinking of the couch in the office next to Richmond Bacon Hadley's cubicle at QCCC. It would be safe enough. Doubtless it would not be up to her notions of creature comfort, but a dose of Quaker simplicity would do her no harm. It had been his bunk all week, but he could yield it for a few days; Hadley or Ferris would put him up.

"It sounds to me," he said, "like somebody was after that envelope more, and knew where to find the two of you. What does thee think was in it?"

She wiped at her eyes with the napkin, grimacing as it came away smeared with her makeup. "Directions?" she mused. "A key? A combination? I don't know."

"Directions to where? A combination to what?"

Her eyes narrowed. "To something, or some place," she said, "where the information was, about why Gil was killed."

She looked triumphant. "That must be it. Information kept safe somewhere. Ray was in the security business, remember?"

two

Penn was still contemplating Ruth's deduction when a bellboy came up behind her chair. "Mrs. O'Connor?"

She flinched. "Yes?"

"There's an urgent call for you." He pulled a small telephone from his jacket pocket. "I can put it through to you here."

"I-all right," she took the handset and held it away from

152

her as if it had a foul odor. The bellboy unreeled a thin cable and plugged it into a wall jack. The plastic number buttons lit up milkily.

"Just press your room number," the bellboy said, moving discreetly out of earshot.

Ruth grimaced and tapped in three digits. "Yes?" she said uncertainly, then frowned up at Penn. "It's for you," she said. "A Philip Gibb. Returning your call, he says."

Penn sat sharply upright and reached eagerly for the phone. But she pulled it back, eyeing him with sudden suspicion. "Who is this person?" she hissed. "And who else do you have following me?"

Penn took the phone. "No one," he hissed back. "But I did tell an old friend where I was going. Hadley's his name-- you'll meet him today." He gestured with the phone. "Somebody needed to know where I was going--what if our killer was hunting for me?"

He bent his face to the instrument. "Phil?"

four

It was early, too early, Monday morning when I realized that Herman Corson had done me another favor. A big one as it turned out.

It didn't sound like it at first. It sounded like what it was, the phone ringing at five forty-five.

My first thought, as I fumbled my way out of an anxious, quickly fading dream, was that it must be Jennifer.

But it was Ferris's non-dulcet tones that jarred me fully out of a too-many beers sleep. I picked up the extension on the floor by the bed and stared at the collection of my dirty socks that surrounded it.

"Adams," he bellowed. "That you? Are you awake?"

I was now. "What?"

"Look, Adams, Herman just called in sick. The mail's real heavy today, and I'm short. I can't let you carry, but if you can come in and case on his route, we could use you, this morning anyway."

We could use you. That's a Postal Service compliment. Probably the closest a postmaster ever gets to an apology to an RCR. But maybe it was an opening to getting my job back, or at least a way of staying out of the alimony slammer. I should have been thrilled.

"Yeah," I said, and it was a croak.

"What?" He growled. "Adams, are you awake?"

I coughed and cleared my throat. The longer I looked at my socks, the more disgusting they appeared. And the farther away Jennifer felt.

"Yeah," I repeated.

five

So at seven-ten, powered by a couple of tylenol and an egg mcmuffin, I was standing at the case for Route 89, a bundle of mail in one hand, searching for Hideaway Lane with the other among the unfamiliar rows of narrow slots, and doing my best to feel lucky to be working.

It was a struggle. On top of everything else, there were two full trays of fat sweepstakes envelopes. Ed McMahon smirked out from every one, assuring several score residents of this corner of South Fairfax by name that he or she might just have won $1,000,000. I was soon so sick of his overfed TV face that if he had walked into the station with a check made out to me, I would have wanted to slug him first. *Take that, Ed, on behalf of all the people you've misled, in part through my labor. and here's another punch, just in reaction against the tedium of it all.*

But he didn't show up. Instead, our first visitor was Janet, an RCR from over at Fairfax Station whom Ferris had borrowed, to carry the mail I was casing. Janet was a slender bleached blonde, with an inch of dark roots and tight jeans, a cowboy shirt, and a salty vocabulary. I saw Ferris eyeing her from his office doorway as she and I were pulling down the mail into trays to load up her jeep. His eyes were narrowed over the red tip of his cigarette.

It wasn't lust I saw in his expression, though, but disdain.

154

I suspected he, like most of the older carriers, had not entirely given up the idea that carrying mail was meant to be a man's job in what was supposed to be a man's world.

They didn't say this out loud, of course, anymore than they said the rural carrier craft was reserved for whites; they knew better. Even so, I had long ago noticed that women rural carriers were few, and nonwhites even fewer.

"Hey!" he called, as Janet hoisted the last tray on one shoulder and clumped toward the dock. "You know where you're goin'?"

She stopped and peered around the end of the tray at him. "Hell yes," she snapped. "Fox Run Shoals to Paddock Lane, right two blocks to Trotting Horse Circle, then just follow the mail."

She sniffed. "Anything else?"

"Watch the side streets," he said. "There's still ice on a lot of 'em."

She gave him what she thought of as a sweet little girl smile. "Sure thing, boss."

Ferris shook his head, blew a tired jet of smoke after her, and returned to his office. I could almost hear him muttering to himself that beggars can't be choosers. But she had answered like a pro.

Janet was hardly out the door when I saw Lemuel Penn at the counter, his expression harried and anxious, asking Andy if Ferris was in. Andy nodded and Penn turned toward the outside door of the office.

I wondered what was up with him. But there was another tray and a half of mail waiting for me, mostly bulk postcards printed with a bright red message about a pre-season summer sale at Woodies, which had to be cased for tomorrow's delivery.

My lower back was feeling sore, from standing and casing all morning, but I picked up a handful of the cards and started hunting for the slots they went in.

Just as I was ready to grab another handful, Ferris reappeared in his doorway. "Adams," he rumbled. "C'mere."

155

"Witnesses?" Ferris was saying to Penn as I came in. "What does she want witnesses for?"

"To establish a solid alibi this time," Penn replied. "I told you about the hotel and Ray Musto." He turned expectantly toward me as he finished.

Ferris looked from Penn to me, then back at Penn. "Yeah," he said with mock reluctance, as if he'd been asked to part with something of only marginal value. "You can take him." He blew cigarette smoke at me. "You're about finished anyway."

"Take me where?" I tried to sound indignant but didn't quite manage it.

Penn spoke up. "Ruth--Mrs. O'Connor called me awhile ago, and asked me to meet her at the house. She says she's figured out something important about her husband's death and wants to show me, and at least one other person. When I saw thee here, I thought thee might want to come."

I searched his face. "Did she say what it was?" If it was that damned yellow slip, I thought, or maybe even the registered parcel, Christ, I'd be clear, I'd--

"Hell, yes," I said. "Lemme get my jacket."

Merle was just coming in from his route as I hurried past his case. "I passed that gal Janet on Fox Run," he was saying to Silas, "I think she's broke down. Ferris'll prob'ly want me to bail 'er out, and I still got me another goddam hour of casing for tomorra 'fore I can go home." When he saw me he called out, "You all finished?"

I walked back toward him, pushing my arms into my jacket. "No," I said, "Penn's going to O'Connor's. Sez his wife's got something important to show 'im. He wants me as a witness."

Behind him, Silas looked up from the clerk's desk, a grin on his long face and the accountables clipboard in hand. "Hey, Perry," he said, "bring back that 4936, and you'll be on the road again." He clicked his pen and began copying numbers on the accountables sheet for the day.

Merle's eyebrows had climbed at my report. Now he reached up, yanked his American Legion off. The overhead lights silvered his thin crewcut.

"A witness?" he shouted. "Be damned if one witness'll be enough." He threw the cap into a half-filled mail tray on the shelf at the bottom of his case. "Hey, I saw Musto splatter all over that freakin ho-tel, and I wanna see this too."

Silas, ever the clerk, was watching him soberly. "But what," he asked, "about your casing?"

Merle's eyes were slits. "Casing?" he spat. He jerked open a drawer under the shelf of his case and pulled out a form. "I'll tell you about *casing.*" He looked toward me, coughed twice, and winked.

"Goddam, Perry," he croaked, "you hear that? All of a sudden, I don't believe I feel so good. I must be comin' down with somethin'."

He strode to the desk, snatched a pencil from a row of three Silas kept sharpened and ready, and scribbled furiously on the form. "There," he said defiantly. "'Here's my goddam Form 3971. I got 472 accrued hours of sick leave, and I'm outta here." He tossed the pencil back on the desk, followed it with the drifting rectangle of paper, picked up his cap and headed for the dock.

Silas called sternly after him. "Merle, you know Form 3971 is supposed to be submitted in duplicate." His voice rose. *"And* it has to be approved by your supervisor." He took a breath. "And what about Janet breaking down?"

Merle's retort was a raised middle finger. "Mr. Penn," he shouted at Ferris's office door, "we'll meet you there. Come on, Perry," he barked at me, "we'll take my jeep."

seven

There were still patches of ice on Bluebird Lane. We followed Penn's Valiant down its slope, and I saw two cars in front of O'Connor's big garage, a silver grey Accord and a black Toyota. Penn parked behind the Accord, and Merle stopped by the wrought iron gate. When I hopped out and took in the scene,

157

my hands suddenly felt empty, as if I ought to be carrying a parcel or a cert. The iron gate had been pushed open.

Penn shuffled cautiously up to us and led the way in. The glass screen door was gone, I noticed. He tapped at the big door, then turned the knob. "Ruth," he called.

"In here," a woman's voice answered. "In the bedroom."

So we trooped down the hall, where there were still bloodstains on the carpet, and found Mrs. O'Connor in the bedroom, dressed in a navy blue pantsuit and a blouse with a big white bow, sitting on the big wide bed.

Her face was as white as the bow, her eyes bulged, and she was trembling. A man stood beside her, pressing the long round barrel of a large pistol up under her chin with his right hand. The round barrel looked like a silencer.

"Come in, gentlemen," he said quietly.

CHAPTER ELEVEN

one

The man was dressed in black: pants, turtleneck, gloves, and a black ski mask. "Move down, Ruth," he said, pulling her toward the end of the bed. Her hands were clenched in her lap; now I saw they had been tied with what looked like phone cord. Then, to us, he said, "Sit next to her." I didn't recognize his voice.

We sat carefully, me next to Ruth, then Merle and Penn, all watching him closely.

"This won't take long," he continued. "It's too bad Mrs. O'Connor insisted on witnesses, because I didn't really want to hurt anyone else. There's been too much bloodshed already, hasn't there, Ruth?"

When she didn't answer, he moved his gloved left hand into her dark hair and pulled her head back and forth in a nodding motion. She whimpered weakly. "Yes," he said, "I thought you'd agree."

Then he spoke to us again, in a tone of mock apology. "My one last hope was for Ruth and I to finish our business before you arrived. But you're too prompt, Mr. Penn. Too prompt for your own good."

He paused a moment, as if in reflection, then I realized his eyes had focussed on me. "But it's good to see you again, Mr. Adams. I've been looking forward to it ever since I lost track of you outside Winchester the other night."

He chuckled when he saw my jaw drop, and then I realized that Ruth wore the same look of amazement. "Oh yes," he said to her, "we were all at the concert together, Ruth. You, Ray Musto, the mailman here, and--who was your date, Mr. Adams? Very striking woman. I was sorry to miss you afterwards.''

I was starting to tremble. I shook my head and didn't answer.

"Well, never mind," he said, "there's business to do, and I'm on a tight schedule. A plane to catch."

He stepped away from Ruth, took the gun barrel from under her chin and waved it in our direction. "You'll all need to sit very still now, while I take care of a couple of things. I'm counting on you for that. Now, Ruth, where is the envelope?"

She lifted her bound hands and gestured toward a large leather purse leaning against the wall, under the framed certificate from St. Joseph's. The man leaned to pick it up, lifted the heavy flap, and extracted an envelope with a red registered sticker on it and one end ripped open.

He held the envelope over the palm of his gun hand, squeezed the edges to open it, and gave it a couple of shakes. What looked like a credit card slid out into his hand.

He dropped the envelope, and pulled on the corner of the framed certificate. It came forward, revealing the round safe opening. He slipped the card into a slot below a keypad, and blue diodes lit up in a tiny window.

"Now, Ruth," he said, "what was your password again?"

"Three," she said, in barely a whisper, "three four two four."

"Of course," he said, punching buttons on the keypad. The diode blinked and I could make out the word "wait" in bright blue. Then a light flashed, the diode blinked again, and he turned the handle on the round safe door.

Pulling it open, he transferred the pistol to his left hand and reached into the dark hole. "Ah, here we are," he murmured, and I could feel the smile behind the mask when his hand came out holding a small box of heavy dark cardboard. The box was just small enough, I could see, to fit into the parcel I had delivered to Gilbert O'Connor a week earlier. When he lifted the top flap, a piece of yellow paper fluttered to the floor.

He glanced down at it, then at me. "Was this something you were looking for?" He picked up the crumpled 4936 and handed it to me. My palm was clammy and the tiny piece of paper felt cold and heavy.

"I wonder why Gil put it in the safe?" he mused. "I suppose just to get the Postal Inspectors on the case too. He was shrewd, Gilbert was. When he slammed the safe door shut, he knew the electronic combination was scheduled to be changed on Tuesday, so if I killed him and took his card it wouldn't work, even with his password."

He pushed the door shut. "That's a very good feature of the security system here," he said admiringly. "I had to get help from Ray Musto to figure that one out. Ray signed for the next card when it came to the office, and he knew you had a passcode too, Ruth, didn't he?"

Ruth shrugged. She was weeping silently, her face puckered, her lips parted. "But don't blame Ray," the man went on, almost as if to comfort her, "he didn't know he was helping me. And when he understood, he didn't want to. Why do you think I had to put him over the balcony?"

Ruth sobbed aloud now. Her head dropped forward, and she lifted her hands, now white under the pressure of the cords, to her face. She gasped and began to sag into me.

"I-I think she's passing out," I said, and reached out reflexively for her. But she slipped from my grasp and started to fall backwards.

"Let her go," the man said, and I sat up again. He stepped past me, stretched out his left arm and slapped her with the gun barrel. "Wake up, Ruth," he said. "It's not time to sleep just yet."

Ruth moaned and her eyes flickered. Blood trickled in a red line from her nostril. On my left, I felt a sudden tensing in Merle's legs.

"Wake up, I said," the man repeated, and drew back to strike her again.

Ruth opened her eyes and started to scream. There was a sudden quivering on my left side and then Merle was on the man, shouting "Hit a woman? You dirty son of a *bitch!*"

Ruth screamed and the gun went off. The big mirror on the wall clanged and splintered, and the ricochet sent the glass

161

patio doors showering in pieces onto the patio.   Merle was struggling with him, and the gun barrel was swinging in my direction. I grabbed it and pushed it away from me. It went off again, and more glass in the doors fell to the floor.

Then Penn was there too, peeling the gun back, out of his fingers, showing remarkable strength.

But the man was lithe and a skilled fighter. Just as Penn got the gun loose, he threw Merle against the wall and stiff-armed me out of his way.

Rolling across the bed, he made a grab at Penn, but the older man was already moving the other way, toward the shattered doors. He stepped through them, glass crunching under his shoes, took one more quick stride across the patio and then heaved the pistol toward the fence. I couldn't see where it went, but the man shoved him aside and ran after it.

"Jesus," Merle gasped, holding his stomach. "that was some pitch, man."

Penn was bending over Ruth. "Used to throw some ball myself," he said. "But he'll find it, and we need to be out of here, now."

"What about her?" I said. Blood was seeping across her face and her hands fell back limply when Penn let go of them.

He shook his head.

two

I was the last one out the big door, and that was good, because I knew to slam and latch the big wrought iron gate behind us, which would slow him down. That bought precious seconds to make for the Jeep, and by the time I had piled in, stumbling over Penn into the cramped back section, Merle had the engine putting and revving.

There were no back seats in these Jeeps, so mail trays could be easily stacked and retrieved. I hunched down, grabbed at the back of Penn's seat when Merle popped the brake to keep my balance, and peered out the big rear window.

"Jesus, there he is!" I shouted. The man ran out the door to the gate and gave the black bars a furious shake. Then he stuck his pistol between them, and I realized with a gasp that I was the best and nearest target. But just as I started to crouch down further, the gun was pulled back. With the Jeep moving away, he couldn't take clear aim from inside the bars. He turned and ran into the house.

"He went back in," I called.

"Good," Merle shouted back. He looked around at me and grinned. "We'll be gone before he can--"

His engine faltered, then stalled.

"You sumbitch!" Merle raged, pounding the steering wheel. "Don't you dare flood on me now, you worthless piece of crap!" I peered over his shoulder as he turned the key and pumped the gas pedal, cursing steadily.

The engine turned over, and turned again. I looked back, and saw a puff of exhaust spurt from under the rear bumper of the Toyota. "He's in his car," I reported, hearing panic in my voice.

The Toyota backed jerkily out from the driveway, and just as I began to wonder whether my chances might be better if I could jump out of this deathtrap and make a run for it, the Jeep's engine caught, and with Merle's profane coaxing, began to move again.

But we were now laboring up the slope of the Bluebird Lane, and the Toyota had infinitely more horsepower than the Jeep, which was twenty years old if it was a day. I felt trapped, paralyzed as the car sped out of the cul de sac and closed rapidly behind us.

The window on the driver's side went down, and the man's arm, and then his masked head came out, pointing the pistol at the Jeep--at me--as he drew nearer. I could see him being deliberate about it, steering deftly with one hand as he aimed with the other. He drives like a good RCR, I thought absurdly.

A figure came into my peripheral vision from the side of the road. It was a woman, wearing a heavy coat and a large floppy hat. She had just pulled open the flap on her mailbox, found nothing, and turned curiously to verify that it was indeed a postal Jeep that had just gone past. She cocked her head to one side, tilting the large floppy hat, as she regarded the peculiar

163

tableau of pursuit being enacted before her.

In some detached corner of my brain I realized that this must be Mrs. Kasabian, because it was her mailbox that was standing open. Behind her, almost out of my sight, her driveway gate was also open.

The pistol jumped and metal rang just above my head, where a bullet had glanced off the corner of the back door.

Merle swore, and swerved a little to the left. I watched as the gun barrel adjusted for this evasive action. I felt I could almost hear the man's thoughts, calmly figuring that the first shot had been quite close to the mark, and the next one would be a bull's eye. Would he aim for my bunched torso, I wondered vaguely? Or maybe try for the gas tank, to finish all three of us in one economical fireball?

The Toyota was less than two car lengths behind us and the round barrel of the pistol looked as big as a manhole. And then all at once the Nazi dogs were on him.

They leaped soundlessly, one tearing at his mask, the other with its teeth in his black glove. The man screamed, the pistol spat toward the sky then spun to the blacktop, and the Toyota veered away from us, into the trees.

I felt the same strange sense of slow-motion detachment as the car bounced down the steep slope, caromed off a tree, and pitched into the pond, upside down.

CHAPTER TWELVE

one

"So who was it?" Ferris demanded, for about the third time.

"I told you," Merle said irritably. "Sanchez. Pablo or Pedro, one o' them. Illegal alien. Don't you watch the news?"

The postmaster's skeptical gaze shifted to me.

I shrugged, as I had before. "He didn't look hispanic to me," I said. "Didn't talk like it either. But what do I know? I was trying not to wet my pants."

Between us on the table sat one of Pizza Hut's bigger pepperoni and mushroom pies, but the only empty wedges in it were on Ferris's side. The beer was welcome, and was not allowed inside the station. But I couldn't fathom why Ferris thought we'd want to unwind from an ordeal barely a day old by eating a concoction that resembled the shooter's face when the Nazi dogs were finished with it. But I kept quiet about that. There was still the matter of my job.

And if the conversation was going in as much of a circle as the pizza, none of us were yet settled enough to be bothered by the fact.

"He was white," I said. "Dark hair, face pretty messed up by the time we pulled him out of the pond and got the ski mask off. But even then, I don't think I ever saw him before, and he was too dead to tell us his name."

I took a long drink of the beer. Something was still bothering me. "What about Penn?" I said to Merle. "Do you think he knew the guy?"

Merle's eyebrows bunched together. "That was peculiar, come to think of it. He didn't say nothin', but he was the one who pulled the ski mask off and went through the guy's pockets."

165

"Yeah. And he insisted we stay there, watch the truck and keep them goddam dogs away, while he went back to the house to call the cops and check on Mrs. O'Connor."

Merle nodded. "He was mighty cool about the whole thing."

"Ruth was lucky as hell, huh?" Ferris said rhetorically.

"Except for being minus a piece of one ear," Merle said. "But I still wonder who them cops was that came and got the truck and all."

"They said something about a special unit--" I muttered.

"Special, your butt," Merle snorted his disgust. "The goddam CIA is more like it. I betcha old O'Connor had crossed the boys in Langley somewhere along the line. Serves him right. Them spook sumbitches don't play."

I shook my head slowly, less in disagreement than in fatigue and confusion. "At least the money was there," I said.

"And the 4936." Ferris was almost grinning at me, and it looked unnatural on him. "Old Inspector Harvard--"

"Harper," I corrected. "That guy never got closer to Harvard than a can of beets."

Ferris smirked again. "Don't be so hard on him, Adams. He's got his job to do too. And anyway, he called me this morning."

This was what I was waiting to hear. "Now that he's happy and we're all off the hook," Ferris said, "you can come back to work." He grinned lugubriously. Bonhomie with carriers and RCRs didn't suit him. "Hell, you can even sleep late tomorrow; come in at seven."

Wow, I thought. A whole extra half hour of shuteye; which I wouldn't get paid for anyway. What a generous guy. "I think I'd rather take a day off," I said, "come in Thursday. There's some stuff I gotta take care of tomorrow."

"Suit yourself. Have some pizza."

"Maybe I will." I pulled a slice loose. Blood-streaked mozzarella surrounded fleshy mushroom chunks and hung in sinewy strands over the edges. I nibbled at it, feeling like a cannibal.

Across the restaurant from us, a man carrying a toddler

166

pushed through the door. A waitress came up to him, and he held up three fingers. A woman came in behind him. She was wearing a tan coat and a scarf, tied under her chin.

Jennifer.

No, it wasn't her. Following her husband and the waitress past our table, the woman's olive skin shone in the light, and wisps of black hair stuck out around the edge of the scarf. As they sat down, she spoke to him softly, in what I guessed was Arabic.

Ferris was checking his watch. Then he reached for his wallet. "I gotta get back," he said.

two

Merle and I were heading to the parking lot when we saw Fred, the driver from Merrifield, coming down the ramp in back of the station. "Hey," he called, "I bin lookin' for you, Henderson."

"Yeh, what for?" Merle adjusted his cap. "What you doin' here when you're off the clock? It better be what I think."

Fred came up to us, grinning around his unlit cigar. "You gotta see this," he said, pulling a buck slip from his shirt pocket. "It's a winner."

Merle grabbed the paper and unfolded it, anticipation creasing his face. Then he frowned. "This ain't my number."

Fred couldn't contain himself. "No," he giggled, "but it's a winner, sure as hell."

Merle rolled his eyes. "Shit." He handed the sheet to me. On it was written 9998.

"That's Ferris's plate," I said.

"Goddam right it is," Fred was doubling over now with mirth. "And-and guess who can collect two hundred and seventy three dollars whenever he's ready."

"Son of a bitch!" Merle snatched the slip from my hand, crushed it and tossed it onto the asphalt.

"Don't be such a hardass, Merle," Fred chortled. "Ferris only plays once a year, and he has me meet him in the Pizza Hut, so it's not on postal property."

167

"By the goddam book," Merle sneered. "That phony bastard. Perry," he punched my shoulder, "will you shut the hell up?"

But I couldn't help it; now I was laughing too.

three

On Thursday, my luck was as notable as Ferris's, but different.

It was raining again when I drove up Jennifer's driveway with a cert. The place was deserted. Peering through the window on the back door, I could see that the room, sparse enough before, was empty.

After looking both ways, I stole quietly around the corner of the house, carefully avoiding the puddles, to the bedroom window. One glance showed that it too was bare. I stared into the space for a moment, as rain dripped off the roof onto my head.

Turning the car around, I was careful going back down the mud-rimmed driveway. Take it slow; nobody back there to help out. That was why I noticed that the flag on the mailbox was halfway up. Was something in it?

Yes: a mailer, a yellowish one with bubble plastic cushioning. Smaller than book size, the kind for mailing small packages. It was light, with no return address.

My name was on the typed address label, with "South Fairfax Post Office" and the zip code under that.

I ripped the packing tape off one end so forcefully that the black audio cassette inside flew out and bounced off the passenger side window. I picked it up, brushed off the lint, and turned it over.

My throat suddenly went dry: "To Perry" was written on the white label, in Jennifer's handwriting.

I banged on the steering wheel in frustration. My boombox player was at home, dammit, and I wasn't even halfway through the route.

Then I remembered that Radio Shack at the South Fairfax Mall was having a spring sale. How could I forget? I had folded and cased almost two hundred circulars that morning announcing it.

four

Packaging for the little tape player and four Size C batteries littered the floorboard on the passenger side when I slipped the cassette into it and pressed the PLAY button.

A moment of silence. I turned the VOLUME knob until the tape hiss was audible.

"Perry, hello," Jennifer's voice boomed, and I quickly turned it back down. "I hope this thing works. Let me see--"

There was a click and a short silence, while she checked. Her voice sounded a little shaky, but maybe it was just the cheap condenser mike in her kitchen shortwave player.

"Forgive me, Perry, but this is the best I can do to say goodbye."

I hit PAUSE. I felt out of breath. I wanted to throw the cassette--no, the whole damned player--out the window. Leaning back against the seat, I gripped the steering wheel, closed my eyes and inhaled slowly. Held it, then exhaled. After ten more slow breaths, I gently released the PAUSE button.

She started to speak again, then hesitated. "I-I heard from Rashid on Sunday. He had just gotten out of the hospital in Beirut. He was shot, at the American University, the night before. A physics professor was kidnapped. He tried to stop it, Perry. His best friend was with him, and he was killed."

She hesitated again, and there was a stifled sound of sobbing.

"Oh, Perry, he's all right, the bullet just grazed him. Fatima says he has a big bandage on his forehead and a black eye, but his appetite is good, and to her that means there can't be any really serious damage." There was a forced, sodden chuckle. "She's probably right, too. A mother knows."

Now her voice deepened, and I recognized the maternal inflections. "The boys were very brave, Perry. Rashid didn't really understand anything except that his father had been hurt and was all right. But Hassan has some memories of trouble in Teheran and Beirut, times when all the grownups were afraid.

169

His eyes were wide, and his face turned pale. But he told his father he was sure Allah would protect him.''

She drew in her breath. ''Afterward, we said special prayers, and they both clung to me for a long time. When I put them to bed, Hassan asked if we were going to go take care of father. I told him, of course we would. What else could I say?

''Perry, when I looked in on them later, Hassan was wide awake. He turned his head toward me when I opened the door. His eyes were so big in the dark. '''Mummy,' he whispered, 'when can we go?' I said we'd go as soon as we could.''

I sensed what was coming next. ''And that means tomorrow, Perry. Thursday morning. As you might imagine, the flights to Beirut aren't crowded these days, so reservations were easy. My parents put the tickets on their credit card. I couldn't have asked them to, but when they heard....'' She trailed off.

''But all this is probably not what you're wanting to hear about, I suppose. You're wondering, what about us, right?''

A deep sigh. ''Perry, I don't regret our time together. You really did cheer me up. But the truth is, that seems like a long time ago now. And this may sound silly to you, but I feel Allah was giving me a kind of vacation from marriage. It was so easy all those afternoons. Yes, you're a great lover, and our talks were wonderful. And I'll never forget the Mendelssohn in Winchester.

''But vacations come to an end. And that octet was our swan song, I guess. Don't laugh at me, Perry, but I'm sure that car behind us, whoever was driving it, was a messenger from Allah. That's why I left. I went to see my parents. I still wonder about it, but if it was Ray, he hadn't told anyone about us. Rashid hadn't even heard Ray was dead. So that didn't make him feel any better.''

I hit PAUSE again. Maybe she was right about Allah; I had seen the driver who chased us, alive and dead, and still didn't know who ''Pablo Sanchez'' really was. I gave PAUSE another click.

''Anyway, Perry, my children have to come first, and it's time for us all to go to Rashid, to Beirut. Call it kismet, however corny that sounds. I can find work there somewhere, and we'll get by. Don't be sad for me. Rashid is a good man at heart, and Fatima won't live forever. Beirut is dangerous, but it's real. For that matter, you'll find somebody soon enough. I'm sure of it."

She stopped, I hoped because the thought of me with someone else was unpleasant. "Still..." she resumed, then faltered again. "Oh, I don't know. Goodbye, Perry." There was a click on the tape.

"No wait," she said again, her voice hurried. "The announcer just said what they're playing after the news. Listen."

Another click. If I'd been smart I would have turned it off right then. But then the strings began, and it was--what else-- The Blue Danube Waltz.

Jesus. I started the wagon, jerked it into gear, and had to swerve to miss an oncoming car as I turned onto Fox Run Shoals. My wipers were working fine in the rain, but still I could hardly see. And I left the goddam tape running, milking Strauss for every last drop of his Viennese schmaltz.

five

Lorena was at the front desk when Lemuel Penn shuffled into Congressman Abernathy's office two weeks later. She was listening attentively to a middle-aged woman in a severe black dress with a white collar and a flattened navy blue hat. The woman, who looked like an old-time school teacher in a silent movie, was closing a venerable leather briefcase.

"All right," she said, as Lorena nodded earnestly, "I'll try again next week. But you must tell the Congressman. There isn't much time."

"Oh, I will," Lorena promised.

As the woman turned to leave, a sheet of paper fluttered to the floor behind her. Penn stooped to pick it up, intending to return it to her. But his attention was diverted by the bold headline at the top of the flyer:

"Eighty-Five Reasons Why the Rapture Will be in 1985."

When he glanced up again, the woman was gone. He swung back toward Lorena. "Really?" he inquired, raising his eyebrows and pointing at the sheet.

171

"For sure." Her smile was bright and confident. "April tenth. No need to worry about sending in your income tax forms this year, Mr. Penn."

"What a shame," he retorted, in mock distress. "It would have to happen when I'm expecting a refund."

Lorena giggled. There was, Penn realized, a new confidence in her countenance which took him aback for a moment. Then he identified one source: her braces were gone. But that was not all; she was clearly learning the congressional ropes.

"Mr. Penn, I'm glad you're back," she enthused. "The Congressman has been waiting to see you. I'll tell him you're here."

She murmured into the phone. There was a rustle behind the partition, then Sue Lee's head appeared from behind it.

More changes: Sue Lee's aviator glasses were gone, replaced by contacts, and her long hair was held in check with a large, rather unfeminist-looking white bow. "Come on back," she said.

Following her toward the inner office, Penn sensed a flurry of motion to his right, beside Sue Lee's large desk. Turning toward it he saw a woman facing away from him, seemingly absorbed in a framed portrait of Robert E. Lee. She had a brown pony tail and was in a tailored pantsuit.

"Right this way," Sue Lee called over her shoulder.

"Just a second, please" Penn murmured. He took a step and tapped the woman on the shoulder. "Barbara?" he asked.

Barbara Keene shuddered as she faced him. She was still next to pretty, but her cheeks were drawn into an anxious smile. Her glasses had also been replaced. "Hello," she said, but her gaze did not meet his.

"Barbara?" Penn repeated. "What--?" He stopped, and his eyes narrowed.

"I work here now," she said nervously. "Well, not actually here. Over at the subcommittee. But it's all part of the same operation, really."

"Yes," Penn murmured thoughtfully. "Yes, it is. Of course." He pursed his lips. "Well," he said finally, "thee

172

earned it, I expect. Passing records to the committee staff."

She looked away again.

"Good luck to thee," Penn said. He moved back toward the inner office.

six

"So," Richard Abernathy said, "what's on your mind, Lem?"

It hadn't taken long to get down to business, Penn reflected. And he understood that the Congressman's celerity was not a compliment. I'm someone to be mollified and moved out, Penn said to himself, to make room for more substantial people and more important matters.

Richard Abernathy was a handsome man. Not a pretty boy--such were automatically suspect in the crisply macho realm of Virginia politics--but craggy and telegenic in a subdued preppy way. His grey eyes seemed slightly squinted, which they were because of near-sightedness. On television, though, he always appeared to be spying out government waste, or peering keenly into the future of the republic, as befitted a tribune of the Old Dominion.

His hair managed to look impeccable but not styled. And there was a scar just above his full upper lip, left by Chinese shrapnel in Korea, small enough not to be disfiguring, but large enough to remind veterans that he was one of them.

Several letters were neatly stacked at one edge of his otherwise clean desktop, with a medium point felt tip pen open on the top sheet. A Harris Tweed jacket hung over one corner of the large chair. His pale pink sleeves were rolled up exactly one fold; his striped tie was loosened just an inch or so.

The effect was a poised informality: in twenty seconds Abernathy could be dashing for the floor when the bell sounded for a vote, but properly turned out in case there were any constituents or TV cameras waiting between there and the Capitol.

"Before I get to business," Penn said, "I wanted to tell thee I was sorry to read of Sgt. Hanrahan's boating accident in the Bay," Penn answered. "Tragic."

"Yes," Abernathy said evenly. "So I read. Did you see

173

it in the *Post?''*

"Not til two days ago. I've been back in the Valley this past week. A friend sent me a copy. It was quite a surprise."

"Really?" Abernathy sounded distracted.

"Yes. And I noticed," Penn continued, "that the obituary did not include a picture."

The intercom on Abernathy's desk beeped, and he picked up the receiver with what seemed to Penn like undue haste. "Yes, Sue?" He listened. "All right, put him through."

He waited another moment, and then his tone was deeper, more formal. "Good morning Mr. Ambassador. Fine, thank you, yourself? Good. Yes, I've also been very concerned about the reports from Nicaragua."

Abernathy raised his free index finger in a sign to Penn to wait. "Yes," he continued, "I'm with you there. The Freedom Fighters need all the help we can give them."

He leaned back in his chair, and swiveled slowly away from Penn and toward the far wall. There a phalanx of framed photographs provided documentary evidence of his proximity to various world-class statesmen, which he contemplated with a slight frown as he talked.

Penn listened for a moment, tapping his fingers silently on the arm of his chair. Then he stood, reached into his inside coat pocket, and unfolded a sheet of paper. Leaning over the desk, he dropped the sheet onto Abernathy's lap.

The Congressman glanced down, then picked up the sheet. "Yes, yes, I agree," he murmured, lifting the sheet near his finely chiseled nose for close inspection.

Abruptly he swiveled back facing his visitor. "Mr. Ambassador," he blurted, "I just had something critical handed to me. I'll need to call you back. Yes, yes. Right away."

He hung up. "What is this? The inscription--"

"Thee knows perfectly well," Penn said. "The inscription is from Proverbs, Chapter Four, in the Latin Vulgate: *'Principium sapientiae,'* 'Wisdom is the principal thing.'"

Abernathy was peering at the image. "It's the motto of Sgt. Hanrahan's prep school, St. Joseph's, in Easton Maryland," Penn said. "Gilbert O'Connor's school too. That's a souvenir key ring that it's on, and those are Hanrahan's keys. I made this copy of it this morning.''

"So what?'' Abernathy was leaning back in the chair, eyes heavy-lidded.

"I took the key ring from Hanrahan's pocket in South Fairfax, two weeks ago,'' Penn said flatly, "after two friends and I pulled his body out of a pond. He had just tried to kill us, and had admitted killing Gilbert O'Connor and Ray Musto. I pressed his fingers against the back of the metal, so his prints are on it. And the keys can all be traced.''

"Again,'' Abernathy deadpanned, so what?''

"The key ring is physical evidence to corroborate our testimony. To prove that Pablo Sanchez, whoever that unfortunate was, was not O'Connor's killer.''

Abernathy's eyes were fully open again. "What testimony?''

Penn smiled faintly. "Whatever testimony we might be called upon to give.''

"Who else has seen these keys?''

"No one yet. But they are in an envelope addressed to the Metro editor of the *Post,* who is a friend of friends of mine, along with some other documents. He would read them, and he would know what to do with them.''

"What other documents?''

"Records of thy investigation into United General and Gilbert O'Connor, which will show among other things that Sgt. Hanrahan was taking bribes from O'Connor while also taping their conversations--''

Abernathy sat up straight. His eyes flashed, and his finger stabbed at Penn. "Gibb, that scumbag. Those came from Gibb. I didn't fire him soon enough.''

"I'm not at liberty to discuss the source of those papers.''

"But you're trying to make it look like I had O'Connor killed,'' Abernathy said. "That'll never fly. We needed him alive and testifying. Hanrahan wanted that money for himself. It was just plain envy and jealousy of an old friend's success.''

"No doubt thee's right,'' Penn countered. "But murder isn't the only crime here. What about the switch of bodies thy cohorts from the CIA or wherever pulled off after I called here from O'Connor's house? It kept a lot of embarrassing connections from being made to thee and the committee and United General in the middle of a Senate campaign. But it can't be legal. I'm no lawyer, but obstruction of justice sounds plausible.''

Abernathy shrugged, a thin smile stretching his lips. "Washington is a rough town. We only did what had to be done.'' He studied Penn for a moment, then sighed. "All right, what do you want? How much?''

Penn rubbed his chin. "About twelve million dollars, I think.''

"What!''Abernathy threw down the paper. "You're nuts! You'll be the one in jail, trying a shakedown like that!''

Now Penn was smirking. "I don't want a penny from thee, Richard Abernathy. That's the amount in thy amendment to the prison construction appropriations bill.''

Abernathy frowned, then remembered. "Martindale. You're going to blackmail me over a dinky minimum security facility? Christ.''

"Not a facility, Richard. A prison. A factory that turns troubled kids into criminals. A warehouse for young men who need something better.''

Abernathy leaned his forehead against the fingers of his right hand. He sighed impatiently. "What do you want?''

"Leave Martindale alone,'' Penn said. "Don't build that, facility. If you must spend the money, put it into drug rehabilitation at the Shenandoah Hospital Center. Or job retraining at Valley State. Put it someplace where it will buy society real protection, the protection of changed lives.''

He pulled another sheet from his coat pocket. "I brought thee a petition about it almost a month ago. And here is proposed legislative language and talking points for alternative projects.''

Abernathy looked at the sheet with evident distaste, and relief crossed his face when the intercom beeped again. He grabbed at the phone. "Sue?'' As he listened, his expression changed rapidly, growing almost feral. "Sure, put him on.''

He swiveled away from Penn again. "Hank,'' he

boomed, "your shop got the scripts for the TV spots? Great! Can't wait to get to them. This afternoon? Sure."

He rotated the chair back to face Penn, who had risen to go. "One minute, Hank," he said, and covered the mouthpiece with long fingers, and held it away from his face. "You know, Penn," he said more quietly, "this makes you no better than the rest of us."

Penn shrugged. "I guess that means it's a deal," he said. "Good. I'll be at the committee markup tomorrow morning, in the back row, just to make sure. And to quote what I just heard, I only did what had to be done. Washington is a rough town, right?"

He stroked the smooth felt rim of his old fedora, and put it on. "But I'd rather quote Scripture, Richard: *'Melior est finis orationis quam principium.'*"

Abernathy blinked at him uncomprehendingly.

"That's 'Better is the end of a thing than the beginning.' Ecclesiastes 7:15. Read it sometime, Richard. Sgt. Hanrahan could have translated it. He might even have understood." He opened the office door.

Abernathy's gaze dropped to the desktop. With his free hand he picked up, then dropped the sheets Penn had left behind. The fingers of the other moved from the mouthpiece.

"Yeah, Hank," he said into it. "I'm right here."